SAM HANNIGAN AND THE LAST DODO

WRITTEN AND ILLUSTRATED BY

ALAN NOLAN

THE O'BRIEN PRESS

DUBLIN

FOR OSCAR AND GRACE

First published 2019 by
The O'Brien Press Ltd,
12 Terenure Road East, Rathgar,
Dublin 6, D06 HD27, Ireland.

Tel: +353 1 4923333;
Fax: +353 1 4922777

Email: books@obrien.ie
Website: www.obrien.ie

The O'Brien Press is a member of Publishing Ireland.

ISBN: 978-1-78849-086-3

7 6 5 4 3 2 1
24 23 22 21 20 19

Editing: The O'Brien Press Limited

Printed and bound by Nørhaven, Denmark.

The paper in this book is produced using pulp from managed forests.

Published in

DUBLIN
UNESCO
City of Literature

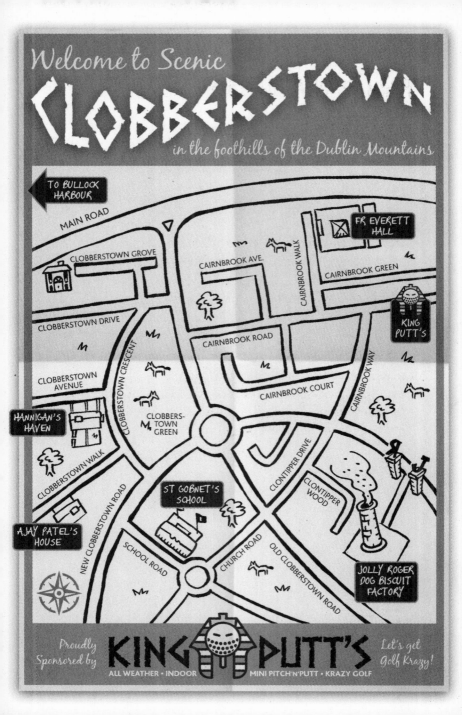

CHAPTER ONE
HANNIGAN'S HAVEN

Plit. Plit plat plit. Plat plit plit.

Sam Hannigan opened the patio doors at the end of the kitchen and stuck her arm out, holding her palm upwards.

Plat plit. Small drops of cold rain plinked onto her hand.

With a happy sigh she pulled on her raincoat and went out into the yard, pulling the patio door across behind her. 'Don't worry, Cecil and Maureen,' she called, 'I'm coming!'

Cecil and Maureen were two new arrivals to Hannigan's Haven, the animal sanctuary that Sam, her granny Nanny Gigg and her best friend Ajay Patel had built at the rear of Sam's family home in the Dublin suburb of Clobberstown. Despite being Capuchin monkeys, which are native to the Amazon rainforest, Cecil and Maureen were not overly fond of rain. In fact, the two small monkeys were found in the neighbouring suburb of Fettercarrig, so they had probably never even seen the Amazon rainforest.

Ogg, the part-time handyman and full-time hulking man-mountain who worked at Hannigan's Haven, had found the little furry creatures two days before, hiding under an abandoned car. On hearing an unusual *EEEEP* coming from under the deserted, rusty automobile, Ogg had hunched down his enormous bulk to peer underneath and found the pair of little monkeys, scared, hungry and clinging to each other.

'Come here, monkeys,' he cooed softly in his deep, rumbling voice, and the creatures crept out and immediately nestled into the fur vest Ogg wore beneath his overalls. For some reason animals instinctively trusted this big, monobrowed human, despite his massive strength and size. Maybe it was because he was almost as hairy as most of them. Ogg brought the two small monkeys straight to Sam at the Haven, and they had named them Cecil and Maureen.

This kind of thing happened quite a lot. Since Sam and Nanny Gigg opened the animal sanctuary a few months before, people regularly brought them stray animals they had found. Sometimes they would be of the everyday, run-of-the-mill types, such as dogs, cats, mice and hamsters, and sometimes they would be a little bit more unusual. Hannigan's Haven was now home to twelve dogs, seven cats, a couple of koala bears, one sloth, one pelican, five parrots, two llamas, a multitude of smaller critters and insects, and, as of two days ago, two Capuchin monkeys.

And – big or small, cuddly or slimy, four-legged or two-winged – Sam loved them all. She adored every single swishy tail, every single pointy ear and every single wiggly tentacle. The only person who loved animals as much as Sam did was Ajay. Ajay was particularly fond of the ones with more than four legs, like cockroaches, spiders, ants and centipedes. But, having said that, he loved snakes too, and snakes had no legs at all. At his own house (and much to his mum's alarm) he kept two snakes, a pet rat and a tarantula spider called Tadhg.

'Monkeys okay?' asked Ogg, peering into the cage over the curly mop of ginger hair on Sam's head.

'I think so,' said Sam, pulling a canvas tarpaulin over the wire mesh on the cage's roof. 'I don't think they like the rain though.'

Ogg grunted and looked up at the sky. 'Better get used to rain,' he said. 'Storm is coming.'

Ogg was right. All morning the weather reports on the radio had been forecasting that Storm Gabby would reach the Dublin area that evening. The news reports were calling Storm Gabby 'The Pest from the West' and predicting high winds, torrential rain and electricity outages. Sam held out her hand again and felt the light pitter-patter of raindrops. She wasn't too sure – it didn't seem that bad so far.

'Ogg will stay tonight, Samantha Hannigan,' boomed Ogg. 'Will sleep in llama enclosure. Just in case animals are scared.'

'Thanks, Ogg. But remember, please don't call me Samantha!' said Sam, who much preferred the shorter version of her name. She watched Ogg as he walked down to the llama enclosure, checking in on the different animals as he passed their cages.

He was such a great friend to have – strong, loyal and trustworthy and always there to help. As well as being a part-time handyman at Hannigan's Haven, Ogg worked full-time as the caretaker at Sam and Ajay's school, St Gobnet's. Some of the younger kids at the school whispered that Ogg was so big and hairy, he might be a caveman in disguise. Sam didn't like that, but Ogg didn't seem to mind. 'Worse things to be than caveman,' he said, winking at Sam.

They checked on Sharon the pelican and Kevin the sloth, making sure their cages were covered and their bedding was dry. 'Ajay will be here soon,' said Sam, looking at her watch. 'He said he'd be over after he fed his snakes. Fancy a cuppa?'

Leaving Ogg to check on the koalas, she trundled into the kitchen and took down a couple of mugs for their tea – a small one for her and a huge one that looked like a bucket with a handle for Ogg. As she was filling up the kettle, she heard a moaning sound coming from the hallway on the other side of the kitchen door. 'OOOOOOOOOOOOOOOOOOOOOOOO,' went the noise, 'OOOOO OOOOOOOOOOOOOOOOOOOOOOOOOOO, my poor finger!'

The door slammed open and in limped Bruno, Sam's older brother, holding up a finger and looking very sorry for himself. His mouth was downturned and his eyebrows were so high on his forehead that they practically reached his curly brown hair. He had wrapped his finger in what looked like three metres of bandage from Nanny Gigg's first aid kit.

'OOOOOOOOOOOOOOOOO,' repeated Bruno, 'my poor, sore finger!'

'If your finger is sore,' asked Sam, 'why are you limping?'

Bruno stopped limping and looked down at his foot. 'Oh,' he said, 'I'm limping because my lace is open.' Now it was Sam's eyebrows' turn to travel upwards. 'I can't tie my lace,' said Bruno pitifully, 'my finger is too sore. I, em, burnt it earlier when I was making a salad for my lunch. Would you tie it for me?' He looked at her pleadingly. 'Pretty please?'

Sam huffed out a *ppppluuurrrffff* with her lips. 'Okay,' she said, 'come over here.'

'No,' said Bruno, limping to the sink, 'do it over here.'

Sam sighed and knelt down to tie Bruno's shoelace, holding one end of the lace in each hand. *Why do big brothers have to be so demanding?* she thought. *And, hold on a minute, how do you burn your finger making a salad?!* She paused mid-knot, but it was too late – Bruno had quietly taken an empty glass from the sink, filled it with water from the tap and quickly but carefully balanced it on the back of Sam's head. Her eyes widened. 'Bruno …' she growled.

Bruno whipped his foot away and, limp now mysteriously gone, danced around the kitchen, cackling. Sam tried to keep as still as possible. The glass of water was balanced on the back of her head; if she moved it would topple and drench her and the kitchen floor!

'Bruno!' she cried, starting to shake with fury and making the glass of water wobble on top of her red curls. 'Get this water off me!'

Bruno just continued to cackle and dance like a loon, loosening the bandage on his finger and waving it around like a gymnast doing a twirly routine with a ribbon. 'Ha ha!' he cried. 'My finger's all better now! It's true what they say – laughter is the best medicine!' He bent down and tied his own shoelace, then he waggled his fingers at Sam. 'Byeeeeeeeeee!'

'Don't go!' shouted Sam. 'Take this glass of water off my head right now, Bruno, I can't move!' But he was gone, his mad chuckles receding down the corridor.

Sam knelt on the floor and fumed. If she moved so much as a muscle the glass of water would tumble and give her her second shower of the day. Just then she heard the front door open and – *PRAISE MOLLY!* – Ajay's voice calling from the hall.

'Hi Sam,' called Ajay. 'Sorry I'm late, I had to feed the snakes and I was waiting for the dead mice to defrost.'

Ajay didn't like feeding the snakes dead mice – he felt sorry for the mice – but it was the only thing Stormbringer and Jeremy would eat.

'In the kitchen!' yelled Sam. 'Come quick!'

Ajay trotted into the kitchen, took one look at Sam kneeling on the floor, and lifted the glass of water off the back of her head. 'Bruno?' he asked.

'Yup,' said Sam through gritted teeth, 'Bruno.'

She got to her feet. This was just the latest in a long line of mean tricks that Bruno had played on her. She had counted six pranks so far that week, and it was only Wednesday. He had started on Monday morning with his signature Early Morning Call, where he set his alarm clock for five minutes before Sam got up, crept up to her bedroom and then ran in and let rip with the noisiest, smelliest fart he could muster, waking her up and forcing her out of bed to open up the windows. Then on Monday afternoon he attached an air-horn to the leg of the chair at her study desk so that it went off with a loud PPPAAAAAARRRRRRPPPPPPP when she sat down to do her homework. Tuesday was a blur of jokes, stunts, larks and mischievous acts of mayhem, the worst of which was when Bruno used some of their granddad Daddy Mike's ultra-sticky Stay-Put Putty to glue the toilet lid closed when Sam was dying for a wee. Sam was so desperate she had to go in the plastic bin beside the sink.

The good news was that today was the start of the summer holidays; they were off school for the whole summer. The even better news was that Bruno was going away for three entire weeks of that summer. Nanny Gigg had booked him into Irish College, and he was leaving that evening for the West of Ireland. Sam looked at her watch. Bruno was due to leave for the train station with Nanny Gigg at four o'clock – that gave her and Ajay just over an hour to come up with a cunning plan to get revenge on him.

She re-boiled the kettle and made two mugs of tea for herself and Ajay, and a giant one for Ogg. She delivered it to the yard, where Ogg was making sure all the enclosures, cages and coops were ship-shape for the arrival of Storm Gabby, then she took out a copy and her pencil case and sat at the kitchen table. 'Right, Ajay,' she said, opening up her copy book to a fresh page, 'I've had enough of being bullied by Bruno. We have to come up with a plan – how can we get payback?'

'Well,' said Ajay, scratching his chin and running his fingers through his jet-black hair, 'he loves his hair – he's always putting gel in it. Could we put glue in the hair gel so his hands stick to his head?'

'Too cruel,' said Sam, although she was snickering at the same time. 'How would he eat if his hands were stuck to his head? He couldn't even pick his nose.' Ajay was right though. Bruno didn't just love his hair, he loved himself. He looked in the mirror so much that until Sam was five she thought her older brother had a twin.

Ajay reached out to the fruit bowl for a banana, and his hand stopped midway. 'Aha!' he cried, swerving around the banana and picking up a hairy brown coconut. 'I think I may have an idea ...'

CHAPTER TWO
MONKEY BUSINESS

At four o'clock Bruno brought his two bags down the stairs to wait for Nanny Gigg, who had promised him a lift to the train station. One bag was full of clothes, shoes, runners, books, and Lamby, the moth-eaten cuddly sheep he'd had since he was a baby. Lamby was once white, but now was a pale brownish colour from years of being dragged around on all sorts of trips; shopping trips, holidays, day trips to the beach and trips to the dentist and doctor. Bruno even brought Lamby on school trips. The other bag, a backpack, was full of sweets, hair gel, and a massive poster of his favourite football team, Shamrock Rovers.

Sam and Ajay burst out of the kitchen, pretending to look flustered. 'Bruno!' Sam said. 'Thank dog we got to you before you left for Irish College!'

Bruno looked at his little sister warily. Sam rarely came looking for him; she usually tried to keep out of his way.

'We need your help!' said Sam, grabbing his arm dramatically.

'Help?' said Bruno with a sneer. 'With what?'

'With this,' said Ajay, holding up the coconut from the fruit bowl. He cradled the hard, brown, hairy fruit in his two hands carefully and gently, as if he were carrying a tiny newborn baby. 'It's a monkey egg.'

'A monkey egg?!' said Bruno, wrinkling his upper lip and his eyebrow at the same time so he looked like he was sucking on a sour sweet. 'That's ridiculous. Monkeys don't lay eggs!'

'In the wild, no,' said Sam, 'but Cecil and Maureen aren't wild monkeys. They never lived in the rainforest. Ogg found them in Fettercarrig – they're local monkeys!'

'And homegrown monkeys lay eggs,' added Ajay. 'Come on, Bruno, everybody knows that.'

'Oh, *yeeaaaah*,' said Bruno, not wanting to admit that he hadn't a clue about monkeys, marsupials or mammals in general. Although he lived in an animal sanctuary, he wasn't that interested in animals, and apart from bringing the odd mouse into school to scare a teacher or two, he really had no use for them.

'This monkey egg,' continued Sam, 'needs to be incubated so the little baby monkey inside can hatch.'

Bruno looked at the egg and then at Sam. 'And you can't do that here?'

'We'd love to,' said Ajay, 'but Cecil and Maureen are Capuchin monkeys, from the rainforest – this egg needs a rainy climate to incubate properly or it'll never hatch!'

'The weather forecast for the next week in Clobberstown is sun, sun, sun,' said Sam.

'And the forecast for the West of Ireland is rain, rain, rain,' said Ajay.

'So you see,' said Sam, 'the egg has a much better chance of hatching if you bring it to Irish College.'

'But why would I do that?' sneered Bruno. 'I don't even like animals! It's bad enough I have to live with them here without bringing them with me to Irish College!'

'But it's only a monkey egg,' said Ajay.

'Yes, and monkey eggs hatch,' said Bruno (who was really quite dense), 'and then I'll be stuck looking after a baby monkey.'

'Aha!' said Sam. 'But consider this: no other person at Irish College will have a baby monkey with them. You'll be the most popular boy in the West of Ireland!'

Bruno, who had been voted most popular boy in the class at
St Gobnet's every year since he started in Junior Infants, liked the idea
of that. At Irish College, kids from all over Ireland would be staying in
dorms, attending classes and going to barn dances every night –
he wouldn't know anyone there and, more importantly, nobody would
know him. The other kids wouldn't realise that he was so popular at
home. What if some other boy from some other town became – *somehow*
– more popular than Bruno? Bruno couldn't allow that to happen.
He would need an edge over the competition, and, thinking about it,
this monkey egg and the resulting cute baby monkey might just be it.
He thought of the wide-eyed, adoring crowd that would gather around
him as, with strong, muscled arms, he held the newborn baby monkey
aloft – just like the baboon *(or was it a mandrill?)* did with the cub
in that famous cartoon movie. *What was it called again*, wondered
Bruno, *the Tiger Prince?*

'I'll do it!' he said suddenly. 'I'll look after the monkey egg!'

'Great!' said Sam, smiling from ear to ear. 'First of all, you will need
to keep the egg wrapped up in warm towels.'

'And bring it to bed with you every night,' said Ajay. 'But don't put
it under the covers – it would be too hot for the egg. Keep it beside you
on the pillow, with the top of the egg peeping out of the towels.'

'You'll need to sing to it too,' said Sam. 'Baby monkeys can hear
sounds when they're still in their eggs. They love to be sung to.'

Bruno carefully took the 'egg' from Ajay and wrapped it in a towel from his backpack. 'I'll sing it my Shamrock Rovers song,' he said, then he held the coconut up to his face. '*The Hoops, the Hoops, up the Hoops, Magic Shamrock Rovers ...*' he cooed softly. 'Don't worry, baby monkey, Uncle Bruno will look after you and make sure you hatch properly.'

'Thanks, Bruno,' said Ajay. 'You really are a monkey's uncle.'

'Nice of you to say so, Ajay,' said Bruno, placing the towel-wrapped coconut into his backpack. 'Nice of you to say so.'

Just then the front door opened and Nanny Gigg swept in. 'Right, Bruno, let's hit the road,' she said. 'It's stopped raining and Big Bertha's all fired up and ready to go!'

Nanny Gigg was Sam and Bruno's granny and had looked after them ever since their parents went to South America for an extended trip to catalogue the tree frogs of the Amazon Basin. She was skinny and a bit wrinklier than most grannies, with curly, frizzy, steel-grey hair that grew skywards off her head in cuckoo kinky corkscrews.

Sam thought Nanny Gigg was the best granny in the world and, although she wasn't big headed (aside from her big hair), so did Nanny Gigg. She had several trophies on the sideboard in their living room that proved it – each said 'World's Greatest Grandma' or 'Supernanny' – and they were given to her by children in the area who weren't even related to her. People, and kids in particular, just seemed to like Nanny Gigg. Kids were crazy about her, mainly because they thought she was a bit crazy herself. And she was. Not put-lettuce-up-your-nose-and-fill-your-socks-with-jellybeans crazy, just a little bit crazy. And they liked her bright, colourful clothes – she had twenty-seven cardigans, in loads of different colours – and her enormous collection of hats.

Nanny Gigg was wearing one of her favourite hats today, a brown leather pilot's helmet with leather ear flaps. She flipped down the hat's fur-trimmed goggles over her crinkly eyes and beckoned to Bruno. 'Get a wiggle on, B-Boy, you don't want to miss the train!'

Bruno picked up his bag and backpack and placed them into the back of Big Bertha, Nanny Gigg's huge amphibious vehicle, which looked like a monster truck mixed with a boat. It was massive and bright yellow, with four orange life rings roped to each side. Its wheels were as big as a tractor's, and it was equally at home in water as it was on land. Nanny Gigg used it for big occasions like grandchildren going to Irish College and fishing holidays in the lakes of County Wicklow. She also used it whenever she didn't fancy taking the bus. This was one of those days.

Bruno grabbed onto a rope and dragged himself into the passenger seat while Ogg helped Nanny Gigg into the driver's seat. 'See ya, suckers!' yelled Bruno over the noise of Big Bertha's engines.

'Don't forget to look after the monkey egg!' shouted Ajay.

'Monkey what?' yelled Nanny Gigg.

'Never mind, Nanny!' shouted Sam.

With a loud revving of the engines and a cry of *TALLY-HOOOOO!* from Nanny Gigg, Big Bertha rolled on her colossal tyres down the road and around the corner, bound for Clobberstown Station. Bruno waved as they went, one hand holding tightly on to the backpack containing what he thought was a real, genuine, honest-to-Gertrude monkey egg.

Sam and Ajay collapsed on the ground in laughter. 'What you do now?' asked Ogg, but the kids just laughed harder, rolling on the grass and holding their tummies like they were being tickled by twenty pink flamingos.

CHAPTER THREE

THUNDERBOLTS AND LIGHTNING (VERY, VERY FRIGHTENING)

The rain became heavier as the night grew darker, and by the time the Clobberstown Avenue street lamps came on, it was pelting down hard enough to rattle the skylights in Hannigan's Haven. Sam and Ajay had helped Ogg secure the animals' pens and cages, but now the wind grew stronger and stronger, making the tarpaulins they had tied over the cages flap loudly.

'Storm Gabby is here,' said Ogg. 'Time to shelter, kiddos. Sleep tight.' With a wave of his massive, hairy arm he walked off to make up his bed beside Gertie and Delilah, the two cowardly llamas, who were already shivering with fear at the sounds of the oncoming storm.

'Thanks for staying tonight,' said Sam to Ajay as they sat down on Nanny Gigg's big tartan sofa in the living room. The wind was howling like a banshee outside the windows and the lights were flickering, dimming and brightening, seemingly of their own accord.

'Tea,' said Nanny Gigg, back from dropping Bruno to the station, 'and I made some cheesy chocolate dippers for the two of you.'

Nanny Gigg was well known for her odd food combinations. She loved cooking but she didn't always pair foods together like other, more normal, grannies would. For instance, one of her favourite main courses was pasta with jelly snakes and parsley sauce; her signature dessert was garlic and radish–flavoured frozen yoghurt; and for casual snacks she served cubes of cheddar cheese on cocktail sticks, covered in melted chocolate and served with a small bowl of crushed porridge oats to dip into – cheesy chocolate dippers.

'It's hard to believe I didn't like these dippers the first time I had them,' said Ajay, dunking his cheese cube into the crushed oats. He stuck the dipper in his mouth and chewed happily. 'But now I think they're yum.'

'They ARE yum,' said Nanny Gigg, smacking her wrinkly lips and reaching for a fourth helping.

All at once there was a loud *ssttizzling* noise as a streak of lightning crossed the dark sky outside the window, lighting up the room with an eerie, stuttering glow. The electric lights in Hannigan's Haven flickered wildly for a few moments. It was followed a few seconds later by a rumbling roll of thunder. In the aviary a couple of parrots started to squawk loudly, and Cecil and Maureen, the two little Capuchin monkeys, began to *EEEEEPPP!* nervously.

Sam stood up and threw her half-eaten cheesy chocolate dipper down onto the dish. 'I'm going to get the monkeys,' she said. 'The poor little things are scared of the storm, they'll have to sleep indoors tonight.'

'All the animals are scared of the storm, chicken,' said Nanny Gigg. 'They can't *all* come into the house. Where would *we* sleep?'

Sam jutted out her freckly chin and looked determined. 'We will find space, we'll just bring in the little ones that are most afraid – they can have Bruno's bed now that he's gone to Irish College.'

Ajay marvelled at Sam. Although she was young, Sam had no problem taking total control of a situation. *Are leaders born to be leaders, or are they made?* thought Ajay. *Or is Sam just Sam?*

The back door was heavy to open because of the wind, but Sam and Ajay pushed it as wide as they could and wiggled out through the small gap. In the yard Ogg was going from pen to enclosure to cage trying to calm down the terrified animals. The rain beat down on Sam and Ajay's heads as hard as pebbles as they trotted towards the koala enclosure, where Ogg was using a wooden club to hammer a plank over the door in a vain effort to keep it shut. The strong wind blew Ogg's long hair, making it wave and swish around like it had a life of its own. 'Cillian and Colin are scared,' said Ogg.

Sam looked through the wire mesh and saw the two grey koala bears huddled in a corner by the potted eucalyptus tree, hugging each other tight. She made a decision. 'Open the cage door back up, Ogg,' she yelled over the noise of the wind. 'We're taking all the animals inside the house!'

'Sleepover!!' shouted Ajay, delighted, and they ran around from cage to coop and from pen to pound, letting each animal out and guiding them towards the back door that Ogg held open with his massive arms. They carried the smaller animals like Egbert the hamster and the guinea pigs in their hands, and brought the really small animals like the mice and the shrews into the kitchen in their cages.

Soon the kitchen and living room were practically vibrating with the cacophonous noise of so many animals shrieking, barking, squawking and *grrraawwwking*.

Nanny Gigg sat on the tartan sofa with her blue budgie Sindy on her shoulder and her fingers in her ears. 'Holy moley,' she said, 'my poor aul ears will never recover!' Sindy took that opportunity to add her voice to the general animal uproar and squawked a loud SKRAAAAWWWWKK in Nanny Gigg's ear. 'Cheese and *crackers*, Sindy,' cried Nanny Gigg. 'You're a feathery fiend!'

Ogg, who had finished up securing the yard, came into the room.
'All animals inside,' he reported, 'except llamas. Too tall for back door.
I will stay with Gertie and Delilah.' With that, he headed back out into
the storm to take care of the two animals he called his 'favourite ladies'.

Sam looked around the living room. The koalas were on the
sideboard, the cats were prowling along the top of the dresser where
Nanny Gigg kept her best plates, and Sharon the pelican was in the corner
watching Rover the goldfish swim in circles around his bowl. *Lucky that
pelican's beak is bigger than the top of the goldfish bowl*, thought Sam,
or Sharon would be having poor Rover as a bedtime snack!

Suddenly there was a crash as a kitten called Lizzie knocked over
a plate decorated with a picture of one of Nanny Gigg's favourite rock
bands, the Slick City Strollers. The plate hit the tiled side of the fireplace
and broke into two halves, turning a four-piece band of big-haired,

guitar-wielding rock heroes into a couple of duos. 'Don't worry, Lizzie,' called Nanny Gigg as she collected the other plates and brought them out to the relative safety of the kitchen, 'it was only a Strollers plate. At least you didn't break one of the Roaming Scones ones, they're my favourites.'

When they had all the animals settled down for the night, Sam and Ajay found a bit of space on the sofa between Priscilla, the huge, yellow python, and Kevin, the black and white furred sloth, and sat down. The wind was still howling, sending gusts of cold air down the chimney, and the rain was beating a rat-a-tat drum pattern on the window panes, but the menagerie of animals inside the house felt safe, and they cooed, bleated softly or snored as they fell asleep.

'Have you decided what you are going to do in the talent show tomorrow, Sam?' asked Ajay in a hushed voice – he didn't want to wake up Kevin.

'Not yet,' said Sam. 'I've been so busy with the animals that I haven't even thought about Clobbertown's Got Tallant yet.'

The talent show was due to be held the next day in Father Everett Hall, and all the kids in Sam and Ajay's school seemed to be entering – partly because they were being forced into it by their parents, who *loved* making them do their 'party pieces' in front of random aunties and uncles, but mostly for the prize money. The cash prize had been put up by local factory owner Roger Fitzmaurice of Jolly Roger™ Dog Biscuits fame, and even Sam had to admit it was a pretty decent chunk of change.

'The prize money would be great for Hannigan's Haven,' said Ajay. 'I'm doing my ventriloquist act – if I win I'm giving the money to Nanny Gigg for the animals.'

Sam was touched. 'Ah, thanks, Ajay,' she said, patting him on the arm. She hadn't the heart to tell him that she didn't think there was even the remotest of remote possibilities that he would win the money. For one thing, his ventriloquist dummy Archie was so old and worn out that its mouth didn't move when it was meant to be speaking. The other thing was that *Ajay's* mouth was a different kettle of fish – it moved when the dummy was meant to be speaking, totally spoiling the illusion. When he had done his ventriloquist act in school, kids roared laughing at Ajay, and not because of the jokes he was making Archie the dummy tell, but because they could plainly see Ajay's lips moving. Ajay never noticed this, though – he just thought the kids were really enjoying the show.

Ajay quietly reached under the sofa and dragged out the old, battered, brown leather suitcase he kept Archie in. Archie had originally belonged to Ajay's dad, Mr Patel. He got it as a child and had brought it with him when he had moved to Ireland twenty years before. It had been second-hand then, so it was no surprise that it was in such a poor

condition now. Ajay opened up the case, took the puppet out and sat it on his knee.

'Poor Archie,' said Sam. 'His hat is battered, his trousers are torn and one of his eyes is missing.'

Ajay sighed. 'He's seen better days, all right. But Dad gave him to me when I was three years old, so he's kind of like a brother to me.'

'Uck,' said Sam, 'hopefully he's not like my brother Bruno!'

Ajay laughed and put Archie back into the big suitcase. 'I was planning to do a bit of practice, but why practise when I'm perfect already?'

Sam patted Ajay's arm again. 'I'm sure you'll be brilliant,' she said. 'Now, I still have to decide what–'

Their conversation was interrupted by a muffled shriek. Some of the animals woke up with a start and there was a fair amount of squawking, whinnying and rustling of feathers. Sam and Ajay hopped up off the sofa as Nanny Gigg came into the living room with Sindy on her shoulder. 'Psssssssssttttt,' she hissed to Sam. 'It'sh my falssthh teeetsh, they're gone!'

Nanny Gigg gazed around the room wildly and started ferreting about behind the sofa, looking for the missing false teeth. 'I jushh maydge mysshelf a schlishe of toasshh,' she said, 'and when I putsh itsh in me gob, I notishhed I couldn't sscheww!'

Ajay looked at Nanny Gigg blankly, so Sam translated. 'She says she made a slice of toast but couldn't eat it because her false teeth were missing!'

Sam and Ajay joined in on the gnasher hunt, searching under tables, lifting up cushions and looking under sleeping animals.

'Hold on,' whispered Ajay, not wanting to wake up the animals that had just fallen back asleep, 'what's that lump in Priscilla's tummy?'

Sam looked at the python who was curled up on the back of the sofa, her long tail hanging over the cushioned arm at the side. She took the snake's large head in her two hands and stretched out her lengthy body a little. Priscilla, who, like most snakes, was a deep sleeper, didn't wake up. *Hmmmm,* thought Sam, *she does seem to have a denture-shaped bump in her middle.*

With small grunts of effort, Sam, Ajay and Nanny Gigg lifted up the sleeping python and brought her into the kitchen. They set her down on the lino and gently stretched her out to her full length. Priscilla was almost two and a half metres long from tip to tail and reached nearly the full length of the kitchen. There was a definite bulge in her tummy. *Could that be the dentures?*

Ajay, who was the most used to dealing with snakes, got onto his knees and inspected the lump with his fingers. Priscilla, still asleep, let out a little hiss that sounded like a giggle. 'It's the teeth, all right,' said Ajay. 'I can feel the molars.'

'Okay,' said Sam. 'How will we get them out?'

Ajay scratched his head. 'Well, we could wait until they come out naturally, if you know what I mean. Snakes poop once a week.'

Nanny Gigg gasped. She ripped off a piece of kitchen roll, picked up a pencil from the table and started to scribble furiously on it. She gave the piece of kitchen roll to Sam.

'NO GOOD,' read Sam aloud. 'TOO LONG. SPARE TEETH AT DENTIST BEING CLEANED, NOT BACK TILL NEXT WEEK. NEED THESE ONES TO EAT!! SORRY FOR KITCHEN ROLL MESSAGE, GOT TIRED OF TRYING TO TALK WITH NO TEETH IN.'

The three of them looked at the sleeping snake. Then Sam's face lit up. 'I've got an idea,' she cried and ran out the kitchen door. They heard her run quickly up the stairs and then heard her footsteps padding around the bedroom directly over the kitchen. Nanny Gigg held up another piece of kitchen roll. 'BRUNO'S ROOM,' read Ajay. *But what could she be looking for there?* he thought.

'Sneezing powder!' said Sam a few seconds later as she came back into the kitchen. 'Bruno always keeps a stash in his bedside locker.' She opened the small paper envelope and sprinkled some of the light-brown powder over the sleeping snake's nostrils. There was a peal of thunder from outside. Priscilla twitched in her sleep. Her snakey snout quivered as she sucked in the sneezing powder. Her long body jerked twice, coiled up into a spring, and then suddenly straightened out like a lamppost as she sneezed a hissy sneeze. Nanny Gigg's false teeth shot out of Priscilla's reptilian mouth and clanged against one of the kitchen presses with a metallic KLANNNGGG!! Sindy the budgie fluttered off Nanny Gigg's shoulder in alarm.

'My densssshurressss!' said Nanny Gigg, picking up the false teeth, running them under the kitchen tap and wiping them dry on the front of her cardigan. She popped them into her mouth. 'Priscilla, that's the

33

second time this month. I don't want to have to say it again: you've two fine fangs of your own, so stay away from my teeth!' Priscilla gave a sheepish hiss and slithered back into the living room.

Sam and Ajay looked out the kitchen window at the storm. The strong, fierce wind was making the bushes in the garden bend over sideways, and huge raindrops were belting against the glass. In the distance they could see Ogg – silhouetted against the lightning flashes in the stormy sky – on top of the llama enclosure, battering some roof felt back into place with the huge wooden club that he always carried. Then he hopped down off the roof of the llama shed and, with a glance over to the kitchen window and a wave of his brawny arm to Sam and Ajay, went back into the enclosure to mind Gertie and Delilah.

The two kids did a last check of the animals in the house to make sure they were all happy and asleep, and then went to their bedrooms, each pulling their blankets high over their heads to block out the loud, thunderous, battering noise of Storm Gabby.

CHAPTER FOUR
EXPRESS DELIVERY!

Sam was woken up the next morning by the sound of soft snoring. Turning her head on her pillow she came face to furry face with Barker, her big, tubby orange dog, who was fast asleep beside her. *Poor petrified pooch*, thought Sam, *she must have come into my room during the night.*

Trying her best not to wake up the dozing doggo, Sam slipped quietly out of her bed and padded over to the window to survey the damage that she was sure Storm Gabby had wrought on Hannigan's Haven. *Weeeeelllllll*, thought Sam, *it could have been worse …* Some of the cages and coops had overturned, one of the branches of the trees had come down into the yard, and there were leaves everywhere, but the roof of the llama enclosure was still intact, thanks to Ogg, and everything else looked fixable – or at least clear-up-able.

There was a knock on her bedroom door and Ajay stuck his head around.

'How was Bruno's bed?' asked Sam.

'Surprisingly comfy,' said Ajay. 'Did you see the damage?'

Sam looked out her window again. 'Yup, it's not too bad – a little bit of tidying up, a couple of whacks with a hammer and Bob's your Auntie, all will be back to normal.'

Just then Nanny Gigg called from the bottom of the stairs, 'SAM! You'd better get down here quick!'

Sam and Ajay arrived in the hallway to find Nanny Gigg standing beside the open front door with a quizzical look on her face.

'What's up, Nanny,' asked Sam, 'more storm damage?'

'I just opened the door to take in the milk from that hunky milkman, Patrick Mustard – you know, the one with the big moustache and the even bigger muscles …' Nanny Gigg sighed and drifted off dreamily until Ajay coughed, rolling his eyes. 'Anyway,' said Nanny Gigg, shaking herself out of her reverie, 'I bent down to pick up the five cartons of milk and the seven yoghurts and found ... this!'

She opened the door wide to reveal a big, cube-shaped brown cardboard box sitting on the doorstep. It was tightly sealed with packaging tape and was as high as Sam's waist. On the top of the box were some round holes and some blue marker writing which read simply 'G.'

'G.' said Ajay. 'Does that stand for Gigg, as in *Nanny* Gigg?'

Suddenly the box stirred, moving a couple of centimetres to the right, then a couple of centimetres to the left. 'There's something inside it!' Sam yelled. 'Something alive! Those holes must be air-holes!'

Nanny Gigg went to the gate and peered up and down Clobberstown Avenue. Not seeing anyone walking away from Hannigan's Haven, or any cars on the road at all, she came back to the door. 'We'd better bring it inside,' she said. 'Maybe it's another poor sick animal, like that crow with the broken wing that Mrs Wilson brought around last week.'

The box moved again, this time jumping nearly a centimetre off the doorstep. 'Whatever's in here doesn't seem too sick to me,' said Sam. 'Ajay, I'll grab the back of the box, you grab the front. We'll bring it into the kitchen.'

With several OOOFs and UGGHs of effort, Sam and Ajay lifted the heavy cardboard box and shuffled into the kitchen. Ajay was walking backwards so Nanny Gigg went ahead, opening doors and making sure he didn't trip over any rugs. The box itself was warm to the touch and there was a faint smell of tropical flowers, like the scent of the fancy fabric conditioner Nanny Gigg used when washing clothes, drifting from the air-holes.

Ogg had been busy that morning shifting all the animals out of the house and back into their cages, coops, corrals and kennels, and was in the kitchen making tea when Nanny Gigg opened the door wide to allow Ajay and Sam totter in with the huge box. 'Ah, Ogg,' said Nanny Gigg, 'be a pet and help Sam and Ajay lift that box onto the table, would you?'

Raising his heavy, hairy unibrow in surprise, Ogg plucked the box from the kids' grip with one strong hand and placed it gently on the table.

The box jumped again, and they heard a muffled squawking noise from inside. 'Who in here?' asked Ogg. 'Will Ogg open?'

'I'll do it,' said Sam. Climbing up on a kitchen chair, she knelt on the table and started to peel back the packaging tape.

'Careful, chicken,' said Nanny Gigg. 'Anything could be in there – it could be a grizzly bear, or a sabre-toothed tiger, or even an elephant!'

Sam looked at her granny. 'I don't think you'd fit an elephant in this box, Nanny, it's not big enough.'

Nanny Gigg put her hands over her mouth as she gasped, 'It's big enough for a baby one!'

Ajay joined Sam on the table and began to peel the packaging tape off the other end. With a tearing sound, both ends of the tape met in the middle and ripped off. The box sat still and quiet on the table for a moment, and then the two sides of the lid sprang open, making Sam and Ajay jump back. From the open box exploded a mass of blue and yellow

feathers, papaya fruits, mangoes, straw and shredded palm leaves.
The mass of feathers grew bigger as it stretched out two large, blue feathery wings and flapped them wildly. Two yellow, scaly feet broke free of the feathers and, to Sam's delight, they were followed by a large friendly-looking head with two big blue eyes and a long yellow and red beak.

'It's a bird!' said Sam with glee. 'Someone has sent us a lovely big bird!' She was a big fan of birds and was tickled pink to have a new one at Hannigan's Haven.

The plump blue bird looked around the kitchen, taking in its surroundings. Then it started to squawk loudly and flap its wings. One slapped Ajay in the face and with a cry he fell backwards off the table, luckily straight into the arms of Ogg. The large bird was now out of its box completely and scrabbling about on the table with its two scaly yellow feet. To Sam it looked about twice the size of an average turkey, but with a much bigger beak. The bird spotted one of the mangoes on the floor and with a loud SQUAWWWWKKK! flapped its wings ineffectually and flopped heavily down onto the kitchen lino. Sindy the budgie returned the squawk from her birdcage on the counter, but the big blue bird ignored her completely and chased the mango with its yellow and red beak as it rolled under the table.

'What kind of bird is it?' asked Ajay. 'I've never seen one like it.' The bird was rolling the mango along with its beak, trying to pin it up against the side of a kitchen press.

'Well, it can't fly,' said Sam. 'Look at the way if flopped down off the table. Its wings are too small to lift a huge bird like that.'

'Those wings weren't too small to give me a good slap in the gob,' said Ajay, rubbing his cheek. 'Whatever that bird is, it's a menace!'

'Ogg,' said Sam, 'any ideas?'

Ogg was a man of few words, but he knew a surprising amount about different wildlife and plants. He thought for a few moments, studying the blue bird as it waddled around the floor proudly with the mango fruit now in its beak. Turning his back on the kids, Ogg reached up to the bookshelves that lined the kitchen walls. He ran his big hairy fingers over the cookbooks, the books on engine repair and the books about the First World War, until he stopped on an old, battered volume with *The Children's Guide to the Flora and Fauna of the Indian Ocean Islands* written in gold foil on the cover.

Taking it down, he flicked through it until he found the page he was looking for, and held out the spread so Sam, Ajay and Nanny Gigg could see. It showed a colour painting of a bird very similar to the one who was sitting on the lino, noisily and messily eating a mango. The bird in the picture had the same blue and yellow feathers, the same yellow, scaly feet, the same yellow and red beak and the same mischievous blue eyes.

'That's it!' said Sam excitedly. 'That's our bird!'

Ogg pointed to the title at the top of the page. 'Dodo,' he said.

'WHAT?!' cried Sam. She snatched the book from Ogg and stared at the painting, then looked hard at the bird on the floor, who was now flapping its wings fruitlessly, trying to get up onto the kitchen counter and at Nanny Gigg's bowl of bananas and apples. 'It does look like a dodo, all right,' she said, then froze, *'but the dodo is EXTINCT!'*

'Well, if it stinks, we'll give it a bath,' said Nanny Gigg.

'No, Nanny,' said Sam, 'it smells fine. Actually, it smells quite nice, sort of fruity. It's just that it shouldn't smell of anything. This bird shouldn't be here at all. The dodo died out over three hundred and fifty years ago!'

The dodo looked up at Sam, shook out its blue and yellow feathers and gave a loud and proud SQUAAAWWWKK!

Dodo

The dodo (*Raphus cucullatus*) was a large, flightless bird that lived on the island of Mauritius, east of Madagascar in the Indian Ocean.

Dodos had no predators, were around one metre tall and walked with a clumsy, waddling gait. They ate nuts, seeds, bulbs and roots, as well as fallen fruit such as papaya and mango, all of which grew in abundance on their safe island home.

The dodo became extinct around 1660, a few years after the island was discovered by explorers – the hungry sailors found the dodo birds very tasty and, because they couldn't fly, very easy to catch.

Yum!

CHAPTER FIVE
DODO OR DON'T DON'T?

Sam, Ajay and Ogg gaped down at the dodo. 'If this bird is meant to be extinct,' said Ajay, 'what's it doing in your kitchen?'

Sam looked up at Ogg, who shrugged his massive shoulders. 'Where did you come from?' she asked the dodo, bending down and tickling under its beak. The dodo squawked quietly and gave an almost cat-like purr. Sam stood up and put her hands on her hips. 'And who sent you to Hannigan's Haven?'

'I think I know!' cried a muffled voice from the table. Sam and Ajay looked around to see Nanny Gigg's pink-slippered feet waving out of the large cardboard box. Then Nanny Gigg's hand emerged, followed by her head. Her steel-grey hair had straw and bits of shredded palm leaves sticking out of it, and she had a green-stained piece of paper

held tight between her dentures. 'I found this in the bottom of the box,' said Nanny Gigg from between clenched teeth, 'under all the straw and half-eaten fruit – it's a letter!' She deftly flipped her small body out of the box and landed on the table.

Nanny Gigg used to be a champion gymnast when she was younger and had a row of trophies and medals on the sideboard in the living room – just like the row of trophies and medals that Sam herself had won for Irish dancing. *Holy moley, she's still got it*, thought Sam, looking at her granny with admiration. Ogg helped Nanny Gigg down off the table, and she unfolded the piece of paper and spread it out on the table.

> Dear Gigg, Please look after this
> bird. His name is Desmond and
> he's a bit of a tricky customer,
> but a great companion. Watch
> out for his beak! Also, watch out
> for those darned animal traders.
> Desmond is pretty rare and much
> sought after. He may be THE VERY
> LAST DODO IN THE WORLD! Hang on
> to him until the weekend and
> I'll pick him up then. I'll contact
> you in the old-fashioned way.
> **M.**

Sam's ginger eyebrows furrowed in thought. 'Who is "M", Nanny Gigg?' she asked her granny.

Nanny Gigg looked puzzled. *Could it be Daddy Mike?* she thought. No, her husband, Daddy Mike, has mysteriously vanished while working on one of his crackpot inventions, way back when Sam and Bruno were little. She hadn't heard from him in years. Suddenly her face lit up. 'Marjorie Crowe!' she cried. 'It's my old friend Marjorie Crowe. That's who the "M" in the letter is, I'm sure of it!' Nanny Gigg sat down on the kitchen chair. 'I haven't seen Marjorie in the longest time.' She had a dreamy look in her eyes. '*Doctor* Marjorie, I should say. We were schoolmates in St Gobnet's when we were nippers. She was always very clever. You would have loved her, Sam – she was always very interested in animals and eco-, ecol-, ecolody.'

'Ecology, Nanny Gigg,' said Sam. 'It means she cared about animals and protecting their environments.' Sam liked the sound of this Doctor Marjorie already.

'If anyone in the world could find a dodo, a bird that is meant to have vanished hundreds of years ago, it would be good old Marjorie Crowe,' said Nanny Gigg.

'Here she is,' said Ajay, holding up his mobile phone. 'I found her on Froogle! It's a news report from last year!' He clicked on the search engine link and read out the news story:

Doctor Marjorie Crowe, explorer and animal conservationist, has been reported missing along with her crew while on an expedition to map the lesser-known islands of the Indian Ocean. Crowe's base camp on the otherwise uninhabited island of Fra'la-la lost contact with her submarine, the *Sea Turtle*, on Tuesday. The sub is believed to have sunk after becoming entangled in the rigging of an underwater shipwreck seventy-two kilometres off the Fra'la-la coast. Rescue attempts are being planned, but the area is very dangerous, being notorious for strong, unpredictable cross-currents and thick fog.

'Marjorie disappeared,' said Nanny Gigg sadly, 'just like Daddy Mike ...'

Ajay looked up from his phone. 'She went missing in the Indian Ocean – the same place dodos came from!'

There was a loud clattering as Ogg pulled Desmond the dodo out of the press where Nanny Gigg kept the pots and pans, sending metal pot lids skittering across the floor. 'Oops,' said Ogg. 'Silly dodo.'

'Okay,' said Sam. 'I guess it's up to us to look after this dodo for the rest of the week.' The others gathered around her as she took charge of the situation. Sam crossed her arms and furrowed her ginger eyebrows. 'Ogg,' she said, 'you find some space for Desmond in the house. He'll be safer inside where those animal traders Marjorie was talking about can't see him. He's a tropical bird, probably likes a warm climate, so maybe clear out some space in the hot press? He can make a nest in there.'

Sam turned to Nanny Gigg. 'Nanny, will you get some straw for Desmond's nest? There's fresh stuff in the llama enclosure. At least there was before the storm hit.'

Sam finally turned to Ajay. 'Ajay and I will go down to the supermarket and see if they have any mango fruits or papay– what are they called?'

'Papayas,' said Ajay, grabbing his coat and a canvas bag-for-life, 'but before we do that, we'd better find Desmond – he's gone!'

Just then there was a tumultuous racket of whinnies, hoots, barks and squawks from the back yard. It seemed like Desmond had found his way out through the dog flap and was noisily introducing himself to the other animals!

A POSTCARD FROM BRUNO

Beannachtai ón Iarthar na hÉireann

Hi Nanny and Ugly Sister,
I am having fun here at Irish college and am not missing you at all. No news on the monkey egg. I've been keeping it warm since I got here but haven't heard an eeep out of it yet. All the other kids love the egg, they laugh and laugh when I tell them what I'm up to. Bruno.

CHAPTER SIX
SEASIDE SPECIAL

All that morning Desmond the dodo caused mayhem with the animals in Hannigan's Haven. He petrified poor Priscilla the python by trotting down the length of her back while she tried to slither away into the garden; he shoved poor Barker out of her dog basket, sending her whimpering off to nap in Sam's bed instead; and he harassed the hamsters by pecking at their hutch with his long yellow and red beak. Desmond even managed to upset the usually placid Delilah the llama by jumping off the top of the chicken coop onto her back and riding her around the back yard like a strange, feathery cowboy on a wacky-looking woolly horse.

'For a bird that's meant to be extinct, he's certainly full of life,' said Sam, watching Desmond as he waddled around the house, opening doors with his beak and squawking loudly.

'Yup,' said Ajay, 'funny how Desmond appeared as soon as Bruno took off – we just got rid of one pest and then another one arrives.'

'Ah, Desmond's so cute, though,' said Sam.

'Cute?' said Ajay. 'He's as fast as a rocket, and I'd watch out for that beak if I were you – it looks dead sharp!'

As if to prove his point Desmond launched himself up the stairs just like the rocket that Ajay said he was. The kids ran up after him, taking two steps at a time. *Cheese and crackers*, thought Ajay, *what's this dodo going to wreck now?*

With a squawk, Desmond barged into Sam's room, flapped his tiny wings and bounded up onto her bed. Using Sam's pillow as a starting block, he raced down her duvet and leaped off the end of the bed, feathers fluttering as he flapped his wings for all he was worth. He managed to actually fly for about a metre and a half before he noisily collided with Sam's bookshelf, sending her books and Irish-dancing trophies crashing to the floor like skittles in a ten-pin bowling alley. Sam groaned.

'Strike!' laughed Ajay. 'He knocked down all of 'em! Game, set and match to Desmond Dodo! Never mind Storm Gabby, Hurricane Desmond is in da house!'

'Hmmmm,' said Sam to herself, picking up the gold and silver trophies and medals she had worked so hard to win. 'Desmond is becoming less cute by the second.'

'That's it!' cried Nanny Gigg, coming into Sam's room with her fingers in her ears. 'I can't take the noise anymore! I'm half deaf in this ear and that bird is giving me an earache in the other one! Come on, Sam and Ajay, we're bringing that delinquent dodo out for some air – a good long walk will tire him out and make him less mischievous. He's going stir crazy in here!'

'Are you sure that's a good idea, Nanny Gigg?' asked Sam. 'Aren't we meant to be keeping him secret from the animal traders?'

Nanny Gigg smiled. 'Don't worry your pretty ginger head,' she said. 'I have the perfect disguise for Desmond.' She held up Bruno's old dinosaur costume.

It was bright green and a bit tattered around the edges, with a dinosaur-shaped hood and a short, scaly dinosaur tail at the back. 'Bruno won't miss this,' said Nanny Gigg. 'He hasn't worn it since he was three years old, so it should be the perfect fit for this feathered fiend. Besides, he's far away in Irish College so what he doesn't know won't hurt him.'

'Or send him into a rage,' said Sam. 'You know, with my old wellies to cover Desmond's birdy feet, this might just work!'

Sam, Ajay and Nanny Gigg spent the next few minutes trying to catch Desmond as he bounced from the bed to the dressing table and back again, making loud squawks that sounded like laughs and smiling broadly with his big yellow and red beak. Eventually he tired out a bit and they were able to hold him down and dress him, first with the dinosaur costume – which covered up most of his feathers – and then with Sam's old pink wellies, which made each of his yellow bird legs look surprisingly human.

Sam pulled the costume's dinosaur-head hood over Desmond's beak. 'You know,' she said, looking at the strange green heap shuffling from welly to welly in front of her, 'from a distance, you might mistake him for a three-year-old child playing dress-up.'

'It'd want to be a very long distance,' said Ajay. 'He looks ridiculous.'

'He's perfect!' cried Nanny Gigg. 'Well, he's good enough anyway. Sam, grab my house keys, we're taking Big Bertha to Bray!'

Sam loved going to the seaside, and Bray was her favourite seaside town. It was only a short drive from Clobberstown and had a lovely beach, a funfair, a cool cliff walk and oodles of places to buy Sam's two favourite foods: ice cream and chips. Her mouth watered at the thought of tasty, greasy chips drenched in tangy vinegar, and delicious, velvety ice cream served in a cone and covered in raspberry sauce. Of course Nanny Gigg, being lightly loopy, sometimes got the orders mixed up and ordered ice cream with vinegar and chips with raspberry sauce, but Sam didn't mind that too much – in fact, in some ways she preferred her ice cream with a dash of vinegar, it gave it a kind of sweet 'n' sour quality.

Nanny Gigg brought Big Bertha around to the front gate. Ajay hopped into the back seat and reached down past the orange life rings that festooned the sides of the massive amphibious yellow truck to haul Sam up into the empty space beside him.

'Where's Desmond?' asked Sam, pulling the seatbelt over herself and clunking the clasp into place.

Ajay motioned with his thumb. 'Up beside Nanny Gigg,' he said. 'Pride of place.'

Desmond the dodo sat in the front passenger seat beside Nanny Gigg, the safety belt across his dinosaur-costumed chest. Nanny Gigg flipped down her fur-lined goggles and revved up Big Bertha's engines, which responded with a mechanical roar. Curtains twitched in some of the facing houses as nosy neighbours peeked out to see what was making all the racket. With an elaborate salute and a shout of BRAAAAAAAYYYY-HO! Nanny Gigg yanked the gearstick into first gear and Big Bertha's six colossal wheels started to roll down Clobberstown Avenue.

Desmond was quiet on the journey to Bray, sitting fairly calmly with his head resting on the side of the truck. He seemed to be enjoying the breeze as it blew down the neck of his dinosaur costume, ruffling the blue and yellow feathers on his broad birdy belly. Nanny Gigg was an expert driver and seemed to know every shortcut between Clobberstown and the coast. She rarely took a main road, driving instead through housing estates, down car-lined crescents and up leafy suburban back roads until they eventually drove over the train crossing at Bray Station and noisily parked Big Bertha in the car park by the seafront. The enormous yellow boat-truck took up four spaces, so Sam hopped down and got four parking tickets from the machine, which Ajay attached to the windscreen using the window wipers. 'Good lads,' said Nanny Gigg. 'Better safe than sorry.'

Between the three of them they hoisted Desmond out of the passenger seat and lowered him down to the ground. Pretty soon he was standing there on his pink-wellied feet, squawking quietly as he looked up and down the long promenade and over the old-fashioned railings to the stony beach and the green-blue sea beyond. Nanny Gigg took off her leather hat and goggles and put on a pair of star-shaped sunglasses. 'Alrighty, then,' she said, 'it's a beautiful day for a walk – let's get this road on the show.'

She's right, thought Sam, *it is a gorgeous day*. The sun was shining, the blue sky was clear, and a lovely cooling breeze was coming in from the sea. People were walking along the lengthy seafront promenade; some by themselves, some holding hands in couples, and some mums were pushing buggies. Sam's eyes brightened as she saw that a few of the people rambling up and down were walking their dogs. She loved all animals, but dogs were her favourite. Her favourite dog was Barker and she immediately felt sorry that she hadn't brought her along; Barker would have loved a long walk in the Bray sunshine. *But Desmond the demented dodo probably needs this walk more than poor Barker,* thought Sam, *so I guess in this case, dodo trumps doggo.*

'Look!' cried Ajay as they walked up the steps from the car park to the promenade. 'They have a funfair!'

Nanny Gigg patted a zipped pocket on the front of her jacket. 'Don't worry, I've brought plenty of coins – we'll all get a go on something!'

Desmond, well disguised in his dinosaur suit, allowed himself to be guided towards the promenade and began to coo softly as the sea air reached his nostrils.

'Ahhhhhh, I love the seaside,' said Nanny Gigg as they walked, three humans and one pink-booted dinosaur-dodo. 'I've been coming here for years. Daddy Mike and I used to love climbing up Bray Head all the way to the top.' She pointed at the huge hill that could be seen sprouting up high into the sky at the far end of the seafront, over the tops of the bouncy castles and rollercoasters of the funfair.

'One time Daddy Mike brought one of his crazy inventions up there, a rocket-powered yoke with big red sails – the Turbo Power High Speed Hang Glider 2000, he called it. It had a metal harness on the underneath and he strapped himself into it. "What are you doin'?" says I. "I'm flyin' back down," says he. And with that he flips a switch on the harness, there's a terrible bang and the Hang Glider takes off like a rocket, straight up in the air and right into the clouds! I couldn't see him for a good five minutes!

'Then he swoops down out of the clouds, laughing like a lunatic. "It works! It works!" he's shouting. He flies past me, knocking my flask of nice fresh tea all over the picnic blanket, and then zooms down toward the beach, does a loop-the-loop and lands on the stones. Doesn't even get his feet wet!' Nanny Gigg took a tissue from her handbag and blew her nose loudly. 'That put me in a right huff, of course – I had to bring the whole picnic basket all the way down the hill by myself!'

Sam and Ajay giggled at this. They loved hearing stories about Sam's granddad and his amazing inventions, and they loved sneaking into the inventing shed that Daddy Mike had built down at the end of the back garden in Clobberstown Lodge and looking at the amazing contraptions that he had left there, all of them covered now in a heavy layer of dust and cobwebs.

'I used to come to Bray way before I was married to Daddy Mike though,' said Nanny Gigg, holding the arm of Desmond's dinosaur costume as he waddled along beside her up the promenade. 'My own mam used to bring me here on the train when I was a little girl and we'd always go to the funfair. We'd go on the waltzers, the chair-o-planes and the rollercoaster. They weren't as fancy as these ones are now, though.'

The crowd on the seafront grew a bit thicker as they got closer to the funfair. They stopped at the first rollercoaster and looked up at the little carriage whizzing up and down the steep inclines and around the sharp curves with a deafening, shrieking noise. The people inside the red metal carriage were shrieking too, some with laughter and some with terror. Desmond started to hop up and down in his pink wellies and squawk excitedly.

'I think our "dinosaur" wants to have a go on this!' said Sam.

'Well, I don't see why he shouldn't have some fun,' said Nanny Gigg, and before Sam could argue, she grabbed Desmond by one of the dinosaur costume's arms and marched up to the ticket booth to buy four tickets. There was only a small queue and after the previous ride had stopped, Sam, Ajay, Nanny Gigg and Desmond got into the carriage, right up at the front. Once they were safely strapped in, the little carriage jolted into life and shuddered up the first steep slope. Sam and Ajay were big rollercoaster fans and loved the feeling of anticipation as they reached the top. Nanny Gigg clung to the safety barrier in front of her with white knuckles and kept her other arm around Desmond. The dodo, who had never been on a rollercoaster before, looked out from under his dinosaur hood, enjoying the view as they ascended higher and higher and *cawwing* at a couple of seagulls as they flew close to the track.

Suddenly, the carriage reached the very top of the slope, teetered there for a second, and then plunged, like an arrow from a bow, down the other side. Everyone in the red rollercoaster car started to scream and laugh as the metal carriage screeched around the tight turns. Desmond was squawking loudly as they went, but his squawks went unnoticed by the other riders – they were screaming too loudly to hear anything but themselves. When the car had done four speedy laps of the rollercoaster, it screeched to a stop and the safety bars went up. People were

whooping with pleasure as they stumbled down the steps to the grass below, but poor Nanny Gigg was looking a little bit green. 'Holy moley,' she said. 'I'd forgotten how fast those things go!'

Sam helped her down the steps and looked back to see how Desmond the dodo was doing. 'Look at Desmond,' she laughed. 'He LOVED it!' Desmond was doing a little dance, jumping up and down in his pink wellies and waggling his dinosaur tail with glee. 'We should bring him on something else!'

'I don't know,' said Ajay. 'This trip was meant to tire him out, not to get him even more excited …'

They brought Desmond on the waltzers, where they were spun around wildly while loud pop music played. Then they brought him on the merry-go-round, which was a bit too gentle and slow-moving for the thrill-loving dodo. They even brought him into the House of Horrors, where, to Sam's surprise, Desmond wasn't frightened by any of the ghosts, vampires or mummies, but got an awful shock when he saw his own dinosaur-clad reflection in the hall of mirrors, squawking loudly until he had to be brought out the back way.

'Sorry about that,' said Nanny Gigg to the staff member who let them out. 'It's my grand-nephew, Desmond – he's, emm, terrified of dinosaurs and, errr, forgot completely that he was dressed as one.'

Poor Desmond was still squawking when they got back into the bright sunlight. 'That dippy dodo,' whispered Ajay, looking around nervously, 'he's going to attract the wrong kind of attention. We have to shut him up.'

'Ice cream!' cried Nanny Gigg. 'He loves papayas and mangoes, so I'm sure he has a sweet tooth. Or at least a sweet beak. We'll get him some ice cream! Come on, kiddos, we'll pay a visit to Mr Softee-Sundae himself, my old pal Mario!' Grabbing Desmond again by the sleeve of his dinosaur costume, Nanny Gigg headed off down the promenade.

'Did you know, Sam, that Mario's granddad, Mario Senior, used to serve me ice cream from his Softee-Sundae van when I was a little girl?' said Nanny Gigg. 'Then when your dad was a little boy, I used to bring him to Bray and Mario's dad, Mario Junior, used to serve *him* ice cream. So now we call the Mario who works in the Softee-Sundae van "Mario Junior *Junior*" – he's the third generation of Marios to sell ice cream in Bray!'

As they walked up to the side of a blue and white ice-cream van, a shiny head popped out of the serving window and a deep voice bellowed, 'Nanny the Giiiiiiiiiiiiggg!'

Nanny Gigg gave Desmond's sleeve to Ajay to hold and then, standing on her tip-toes, reached up and hugged Mario Junior Junior, who was precariously hanging out of the ice-cream van.

'Is been a long time,' said Mario Junior Junior. 'How come you no come see Mario Junior Junior no more, eh?'

Nanny Gigg laughed. 'Mario, I was here last month with the girls on the Bingo Bus, don't you remember?' She turned to Sam and Ajay and whispered, 'Mario's memory isn't the best – I think he has brain-freeze from all the ice cream he eats.'

'Ah yes! I remember now!' said Mario. 'So good to see you, Nanny the Gigg. Aren't you going to introduce me to your short friends?'

'This is Sam and Ajay,' said Nanny Gigg, 'and the small green one is my, ehhhh, little grand-nephew, Desmond.'

'So please to meet!' said Mario Junior Junior. 'Now, what ice cream you all like? The usual for you, Nanny the Gigg? On the house! Or should I say, on the van!'

Nanny Gigg was delighted – she loved free stuff – and ordered ice-cream cones with raspberry sauce for the kids and the dodo, and the usual, an ice-cream cone with a chocolate flake, for herself. 'Thank you so much, Mario,' she said as she took the ice creams and handed them out to Sam and Ajay. 'You're a good boy and the Softee-Sundae van looks great. Mario Senior and Mario Junior would be very proud. Tell them I said *hello* next time you see them!'

They sat down on the wall to eat their ice creams, and three large seagulls immediately swooped down to land near their feet. 'Watch out for those greedy fellas,' said Nanny Gigg. 'They'll be after the scraps from your cones.'

Ajay polished off his ice cream quickly so he could hold Desmond's cone for him. The dodo was hopping up and down in his dinosaur costume in excitement and, after a sniff of the cone with his beak, swallowed the whole ice cream in two gulps. 'I think we can safely say he loved that,' said Ajay, watching the big bird as he flopped down onto the ground and let out a satisfied *squawwwwk*.

'Nanny Gigg,' said Sam. 'Why do you always get a chocolate flake in your ice cream?'

Nanny Gigg slurped up the last of her ice cream and bit into her cone with her big false teeth. 'Because,' she said, crunching away merrily on the wafer, 'if any of those greedy seagulls come flying towards me trying to whip the ice cream out of my hand, I'd have a weapon to fight them off – I'd batter them with my chocolate flake! Right-ho, bouncy castle next!'

Their go on the blue bouncy castle with octopuses painted on the side was cut short, however, when Desmond the dodo, who was bouncing along happily beside Sam, Ajay and Nanny Gigg, managed to puncture the rubber floor with his beak. There was a whooshing noise as the air started to escape and the walls began to deflate on either side of them, collapsing in slow motion. 'This dopey dodo is going to get us all into trouble,' said Ajay, looking around nervously for the bouncy castle attendant.

'Don't worry!' cried Nanny Gigg. 'I have some Ultra Strong Denture Fixative with me. Daddy Mike invented it for keeping my false teeth in on windy days. If it works on my big gob of teeth, it'll work a treat on this bouncy castle!' She grabbed the two sides of the tear in the rubber floor and, holding them together with one hand, spread the glue-like fixative over them with the other. The hissing, whooshing sound immediately stopped. 'Told ya!' she said brightly. 'Now, let's get off this rubbery yoke and get some dinner.'

Sam wanted to complain that they'd just had dessert, but she knew Nanny Gigg was as prone to mixing up meal courses as she was to mixing up ingredients. On several occasions she had served up soup to Sam a whole hour after she had finished her main course, and half an hour *after* she had gone to bed. Besides all that, Sam was still hungry and the smell from the chip shops was drifting up from the far end of the promenade and making her mouth water.

With a much quieter Desmond in tow, the kids and Nanny Gigg wandered down to the food vans, checking out their brightly coloured menus and savouring the aromas as they passed by.

None of them paid much attention to the cream and red coloured van that was parked a little away from the others, and only Ajay glanced for a moment at its big, neon sign that read 'The Greedy Gourmand'. He paused long enough to notice the black smoke that belched out of a thin chimney that sprouted out of the van's roof like a wild, poisonous toadstool, and then he moved on, trotting a little to catch up with Sam, Desmond and Nanny Gigg, who had stopped at a falafel stall. Ajay hadn't noticed at all the big satellite dish on the Greedy Gourmand's roof that came to life and swiveled slowly in his direction, or the small head with the chef's hat that poked suddenly out of the driver's window.

OOOOHHH JANEY, IT'S...
CAPTAIN STINKY & CHUM

CAPTAIN STINKY DERRIÈRE, OWNER OF THE GREEDY GOURMAND, PART-TIME ANIMAL POACHER, FULL-TIME GLUTTON.

MISTER CHUM, STINKY'S SOUS-CHEF/ SLIGHTLY EVIL HENCHMAN.

FOO-FOO, CHUM'S CHIHUAHUA-POODLE, RECORD HOLDER FOR THE TEENIEST DOG IN IRELAND.

LET US GO TO THE DEV-, I MEAN, THE DINING ROOM. I 'AVE SOME NEWS ZAT I AM VERRRRY EXCITED ABOUT.

MY RARE ANIMAL DETECTOR EQUIPMENT 'AS PICKED UP AN UNUSUAL SCENT ...

... AS HAS MY PARTICULARLY EXTRAORDINARY NOSE.

VOILÀ! WITH ZE SATELLITE DISH ON ZE ROOF OF ZE VAN WE ARE TRACKING ZIS SCENT!

MONSIEUR CHUM, YOU KNOW 'OW I LOVE FOOD ...

AND 'OW I 'AVE A TASTE FOR ZE UNUSUAL, ZE RARE, ZE FREAKISHLY DELICIOUS?

DO YOU REMEMBER ZE FIRST TIME I TASTED ZE - 'OW YOU SAY - ZE FOOD ZAT OTHER PEOPLE TURN THEIR NOSES UP TO?

HOW COULD I FORGET, CAPTAIN? I HAD JUST STARTED AS A CHEF ...

TEN YEARS EARLIER ...

CHUM, VOUS *IMBECILE!*

WHEN I TOLD YOU TO MAKE RATATOUILLE, I DID NOT EXPECT YOU TO MAKE IT WITH A REAL RAT!

I AM SORRY, HEAD CHEF, THERE ARE JUST SO MANY RATS IN THIS KITCHEN, I THOUGHT THAT WAS WHAT YOU WANTED. WILL I THROW IT AWAY?

NO! WE WILL GIVE IT TO OUR IDIOT CUSTOMERS, ZEY WILL NOT KNOW ZE DIFFERENCE.

HMMM. ON ZE OTHER HAND, KEEP ZIS RATATOUILLE FOR ME - ZE RAT HAS MADE ZIS DISH DEEE-LISH!

68

YUM ... SINCE ZAT DAY, MONSIEUR CHUM, I HAVE MADE IT MY LIFE'S MISSION TO TRAVEL ZE WORLD AND TO EAT *ALL* ZE ANIMALS - *ALL* ZE DELICIOUS MEAT - ZAT NORMAL, EVERYDAY, BORING PEOPLE DO NOT.

I 'AVE EATEN BARBECUED BEARS IN BERLIN, I 'AVE EATEN MARINATED MOLES IN MINSK ...

... I 'AVE EVEN NIBBLED ON PURÉED PYTHON IN PEKING.

ALL 'AVE TASTED DELICIOUS AND ALL 'AVE SMELLED DELECTABLE. BUT NONE 'AVE 'AD ZE DELIGHTFUL, MOUTH-WATERING, UNIQUE ODOUR SUCH AS ZE ONE I SMELLED TODAY.

MONSIEUR CHUM, IF I AM NOT VERRRY MUCH MISTAKEN, I THINK WE MAY HAVE FOUND ZE MOST PRECIOUS AND RARE ANIMAL OF ALL ... A BIRD SO RARE IT IS THOUGHT TO HAVE A LONG TIME AGO KICKED ZE BUCKET, SO RARE IT IS UNDOUBTEDLY EXTINCT!

DOESN'T IT SMELL JUST SOOOOOO DE-DODO-LICIOUS?

EXTINCT

Dodo

The dodo (*Raphus cucullatus*) was a large, flightless bird that lived on the island of Mauritius, east of Madagascar in the [ ] Ocean.

Do [ ] one [ ] waddling [ ] any [ ] as [ ]

[ ]ators, were around [ ]ked with a clumsy, [ ]uts, seeds, bulbs [ ] fruit such as papaya [ ] in abundance

[ ]nd 1660, a few years [ ] by explorers – the [ ]ds very tasty and, [ ] to catch.

CHAPTER SEVEN
CLOBBERSTOWN'S GOT TALLANT?

Desmond the dodo was much less mischievous the next day. He had a good sleep in the nest that Ogg had prepared for him in the space under the stairs and woke up the following morning in good form, squawking for food. As Nanny Gigg sliced up some papayas for his breakfast, Desmond waddled upstairs and stopped just outside Sam's bedroom door, cocking his head sideways to listen. Sam was in her bedroom with Ajay, who had come back over to Hannigan's Haven early that morning to practise for the afternoon's talent show. Ajay clicked open the lid of his big brown battered leather suitcase, took his ventriloquist dummy Archie out and polished the puppet's head with a hanky. 'So,' he said to Sam, 'how are you getting on with your act?'

'What act?' said Sam. 'I haven't been able to figure out what to do yet!'

Ajay smiled and sat Archie up on his knee. 'Ajay gight hab an igea,' he made the puppet say in a funny, squeaky voice.

'Sorry, what was that?' said Sam. Ajay's ventriloquist act wasn't improving – Sam couldn't understand him at all unless he was moving his lips, and not moving your lips while making the dummy talk was the most important part of ventriloquism. *Poor Ajay*, she thought. *He's a terrible ventriloquist – he's never going to win Clobberstown's Got Tallant.*

'I said,' said Ajay, laying down the dummy on the bed and speaking in his normal voice, 'Ajay might have an idea!'

He picked up his jacket off the bed and, reaching into the inside pocket, took out a gold-coloured musical instrument with a round, bulbous shape at one end, a mouthpiece at the top and two pipes coming out underneath. Each pipe had a row of small finger holes. 'It's called a pungi,' said Ajay. 'Dad found it in a music shop in town. You blow in here and move your fingers on the two pipes to make notes.' Ajay blew into the mouthpiece and played a few notes. The sound was clear, sweet and a little wistful. 'It's easy enough to use,' he said. 'It's like playing two tin whistles at the same time!'

He handed the pungi to Sam, who gave it a tentative toot. 'I'll never be able to learn how to play "The Walls of Limerick" on this by this afternoon,' she said, moving her fingers up and down the two pipes.

'You don't have to play a tune on it!' said Ajay, laughing. 'The pungi is also known as the snake charmer's flute – I thought you could bring Priscilla the python on stage in the great big wicker laundry basket Nanny Gigg has in the bathroom, and get her to rise up out of the basket when you play a few notes on the flute.'

Sam raised her eyebrows. 'Nanny Gigg would never get into the laundry basket!'

'Not Nanny Gigg – the snake!' Ajay laughed so hard he fell off the bed. 'Priscilla would be in the basket. You come out wearing a turban and charm the snake out. It's a snake-charmer act! We could train Priscilla this morning. Snakes love the sound of the pungi, they sway from side to side to the notes – it looks like they're dancing to the music!'

'Hmmm,' said Sam. 'I'm pretty sure Nanny Gigg has a purple turban in her bedroom. She has a huge collection of hats in there.'

Ajay clapped his hands together. 'I'll help you,' he said. 'My ventriloquist act is perfect, so I've plenty of time!'

They brought Priscilla up to the bedroom and tried all morning to train her, but the huge python wasn't very cooperative. She ignored the sound of the snake charmer's pungi completely, preferring to either coil herself up and take a nap, or go for a little slither around the bedroom.

She particularly liked nosing around under Sam's bed. 'There's probably a mouse under there,' said Ajay. 'Maybe she's hungry?'

Sam looked at the alarm clock on her bedside table. 'She's always hungry,' she said. 'It's almost two o'clock, Ajay. The snake's not ready, but we've run out of time. We better put her in the laundry basket and get around to the hall.'

'It'll be all right on the night,' said Ajay. 'You'll be fine once you and Priscilla get on stage – these things have a way of working out.'

Sam wasn't too sure. Her snake-charmer act had DISASTER written all over it in big letters, and, despite his optimism, Sam thought that Ajay's dummy act could turn out to be a bit of a dead duck too. She didn't say this to Ajay, of course – he was her best friend and she didn't want to hurt his feelings. *Maybe I should have just done my Irish dancing again*, she thought, *like I did last year ... and the year before that ... and the year before that ...*

While Ajay wrestled Priscilla into the large wicker laundry basket, Sam went downstairs to ask Nanny Gigg if she could borrow her turban. She found her granny chasing the dodo in circles around the kitchen table. 'Desmond!' Nanny Gigg was yelling. 'Give me back my cheese sandwich!'

Desmond made a break for the door as Sam opened it and dived past her in a flurry of blue and yellow feathers, nearly bowling her over. Sam hung onto the door frame as the big bird dashed up the stairs, a half-eaten cheese sandwich in its beak and a rascally look in its eye.

'That bird is as bold as brass!' said Nanny Gigg, leaning up against the kitchen worktop and wheezing. 'The weekend can't come quick enough!'

After they had retrieved Nanny Gigg's purple turban hat from her bedroom, she and Sam helped Ajay heave the heavy, snake-filled wicker basket down the stairs. 'Dad is coming to pick us up any second now,' said Ajay, looking at his watch. There was a ring at the doorbell. 'What did I tell you?' said Ajay, triumphantly. He was very proud of his dad, 'the bestest, most on-time taxi man in Clobberstown!' With Mr Patel's help, Sam and Ajay bundled the basket into the boot of the taxi, and then Ajay went back inside the house to get his suitcase from Sam's bedroom. He was met at the hall door by Nanny Gigg.

'I can't find that dumb dodo,' she said, looking a little frazzled. 'I found the crusts off my cheese sandwich upstairs on the landing, but there's no sign of that dratted Desmond!'

Ajay looked at his watch again. They were cutting it fine if they wanted to be at the talent show on time. 'Would you like us to help look for him?' he said.

'No, chicken,' said Nanny Gigg. 'I'll look for him. He's probably hiding under a bed. Not that he'd fit under one – he's a whopper of a bird. You and Sam go on ahead, I'll follow you on the bus and see you there!'

Ajay ran upstairs and, clicking the big lid closed on his old leather suitcase, dragged it downstairs and out to the car. *Holy moley*, he thought, *shifting that python down the stairs must have tired me out – this suitcase feels very heavy!* He got into the back seat beside Sam, clicked in his seatbelt, and Ajay's dad took off for the short journey to Father Everett Hall.

The hall was covered in colourful bunting and a long banner on the gates read *CLOBBERSTOWN'S GOT TALLANT – PROUDLY SPONSORED BY JOLLY ROGER™ DOG BISCUITS.*

'They've spelled "talent" wrong,' said Ajay's dad, pulling up the taxi as close to the gate as he could. 'I'm glad it's a talent show and not a spelling bee.'

Sam and Ajay hopped out, and Mr Patel opened the boot and hefted out the wicker laundry basket and the battered brown suitcase, wheezing as he did so. 'What have you got in here, Ajay,' asked his dad, 'concrete blocks?'

Ajay grabbed the handle of the case and dragged it onto the path. It really did feel heavy.

'Thanks, Sanjeev,' said Sam. 'See you after the show!'

Ajay's dad handed his son a large paper bag from the front seat, and with a quick shout of 'Good luck!' and a beep of the horn, he drove off.

With some huffing and puffing, Sam and Ajay tugged the wicker basket and the leather suitcase into the hall and up to the registration desk. They signed in and got their competitor numbers and registration cards, then dragged their two heavy loads around the side of the curtains to the dressing room behind the stage. The room was lined with mirrors and jam-packed with kids. Some of the kids were holding musical instruments and were blowing into them, plucking at them or strumming the strings of them noisily. Others were dressed in gymnastic gear or hip-hop outfits and were elbowing each other in the small, cramped room for space to practice.

Ajay and Sam backed out into the hallway, away from the cacophonous noise and the pointy elbows. 'I'll get changed in the toilets,' said Ajay. 'Mind my suitcase.' He took the paper bag his dad had given him, and, within a couple of minutes, came out of the loo wearing a long blue duffle coat and a floppy, wide-brimmed brown hat.

'You look like Paddington Bear!' laughed Sam, pulling on her granny's purple turban.

'Nanny Gigg's head must be much bigger than yours,' said Ajay. 'That hat is huge on you – you look like a big purple lollipop!'

The show started at three o'clock on the dot and, one by one, the acts were herded onto the stage to a smattering of applause from the crowd of children, proud mums, dads, aunties, uncles and grandparents. Martha Maguire and Abbie Cuffe, two girls from Sam and Ajay's class, were up first. After being introduced by local legend Patrick Mustard, the moustachioed milkman, who was acting as MC for the afternoon, they performed an Irish dancing reel. They went down well, but Pat Mustard seemed to get a bigger cheer than the girls did, especially from the grannies in the audience.

The next act was a teenager who, despite the dark of the hall, was wearing sunglasses as she strutted onto the stage. She insisted on being called 'just Chloë' because, she reasoned, all the best singers only have the one name, like Cher or Beyoncé. Unfortunately for Chloë, and the audience, her off-tune singing sounded nothing like Beyoncé *or* Cher. 'That's why she has no second name and wears shades,' whispered Ajay to Sam. 'She doesn't want to be recognised for her crimes against music.'

After a few more acts of varying quality – including an elderly man who juggled clocks while bellowing 'It's TIME for juggling!' and a small girl dressed up as President Michael D Higgins who read poetry – it was Sam's turn. Wearing her granny's purple turban, she dragged the heavy wicker laundry basket containing Priscilla the python onto the stage. She handed her registration card to Patrick the milkman, who glanced at it and said into the microphone, 'And now, ladles and jellyspoons, blobs and grills, we have Clobberstown's own Sam Hannigan, who is going to entertain us all with some' – he squinted at the card – 'snake farming!'

Sam stood on her tip-toes and shouted into the microphone, 'That's snake *charming!*' One person in the audience started to clap wildly and stamp their feet. *Ahhh*, thought Sam, *Nanny Gigg has arrived then!*

Patrick stood back and Sam sat on the floor beside the big wicker basket, her legs crossed. She took out the pungi pipes and, pushing the too-big turban back up off her face, started to play some long, haunting notes. There was no movement from the basket. She had hoped that Priscilla, even if she wasn't going to sway from side to side to the music like Ajay had said, would at least show her face.

Sam got closer to the side of the basket, just in case Priscilla couldn't hear, and blew the pungi a few more times, much louder this time. She blew so hard she jerked the flute up on the last note and knocked it off the basket. The tall basket teetered and tottered and then fell sideways on the stage, the circular lid detaching and rolling behind the curtains, into the wings. Sam jumped to her feet. There was a hissing noise and Priscilla the python took that opportunity to make an appearance after all, slithering her long body out of the overturned basket and sliding across the stage, where she waved her snakey head at the kids in the front row. The children, and a number of the dads, leaped from their seats in fright, pelting the rows behind with a shower of popcorn and jelly babies.

Despite Sam grabbing the microphone from Patrick and trying to calm the crowd by telling them that Priscilla was a friendly python who wouldn't harm a fly, it was several minutes before order was restored to the hall. After the huge python was safely put back into the basket and the lid secured in place with duct tape, the front row resumed their seats, all the time throwing dirty looks in Sam's direction.

'What a disaster!' said Sam grimly as she came backstage and pulled off the purple turban. 'I have a feeling that Priscilla and I may not have won the prize. Or made any new friends, especially in the front row. It's up to you now, Ajay.' She clapped him on the back of his blue duffle coat. 'Just remember, no matter how bad you are, you couldn't do worse than I did. Go get 'em, Paddington!'

Just then Ajay's number was called and, with a quick thumbs-up to Sam, he pulled his heavy brown leather suitcase onto the stage.

'Janey mackers, snakes on a stage?' Patrick the milkman was saying to the audience. 'You know, they say a nice big cup of milky tea is good for a shock – the milkier the better!'

A few people tittered nervously at this, still getting over the shock of coming face-to-face with a real, live python, but Ajay could hear Nanny Gigg's loud guffaws coming from the back of the hall.

'Next up,' said Patrick, 'we have young ventril- ventkwik- ventrol-, ahem, puppet person, Ajay Patel!'

Ajay looked into the audience but couldn't make out where Nanny Gigg was sitting – he couldn't see anyone beyond the second row because of the spotlight shining on his face. He shrugged, turned his back on the audience and bent down to open the huge battered suitcase. The audience broke out in laughter at the sight of his blue, duffle-coated behind sticking up in the air. Ajay, puzzled, looked around wearing his brown, floppy brimmed hat, and the audience laughed even louder. *Hmmmm*, thought Ajay, *this is going great – the crowd loves me!*

He turned back to the suitcase, clicked the fasteners and flipped open the lid. He gasped. Inside the case, where he had expected to find Archie, his trusty though slightly wonky, tramp-like ventriloquist dummy, was sitting a huge ball of blue and yellow feathers. Horror dawned in Ajay's wide eyes as a scaly yellow foot appeared from the feathery bundle, followed by a yellow and red beak.

'Desmond,' whispered Ajay, 'that's where you got to! What have you done with Archie?' He glanced back at the audience who were quiet now, waiting for the act to begin, and was glad he was wearing the oversized duffle coat – it blocked them from seeing the holy-moley-aren't-they-meant-to-be-extinct dodo. Ajay reached under the big bird, looking in vain for his puppet, but Desmond pecked at him with his beak. 'Okay,' he said, thinking quickly, 'there's only one way out of this. Desmond, if you stay still and cooperate, I'll go to the supermarket and get you the biggest mango you've ever seen.' Desmond gave a quiet squawk.

Before he could change his mind, Ajay hoisted Desmond the dodo out of the suitcase with a loud grunt of effort. He slammed the lid shut and sat down on the case with the large bird on his knee. There were *oohs* and *aahs* from the crowd. 'What a beautiful puppet!' whispered one old lady. 'Aren't those feathers only gorgeous?' murmured another.

Ajay coughed nervously. He caught sight of Sam standing at the side of the stage. She had her hands up to her mouth and a very panicked look on her face. 'Ladies and gentlemen,' he said, 'my name is Ajay and this is Arch– I mean, this is Desmond the, er, duck? Yes, Desmond the duck, that's his name! We are going to tell you some jokes, aren't we Desmond?'

At this point in the act Ajay would make Archie the ventriloquist dummy answer back that yes indeed, they were going to tell the audience some jokes. Ajay made Archie speak by pulling a lever hidden inside the dummy's back. Unfortunately dodos don't have levers. In desperation, Ajay squeezed the back of the dodo's neck softly and, to Ajay's combined astonishment and relief, Desmond opened his beak and gave the quietest squawk he had ever given.

'YUSS,' said Ajay, his lips rigid and his teeth clenched. The audience laughed, which gave Ajay a bit of a boost – they might just get through this after all!

Ajay coughed again. 'I say, I say, I say,' he said to Desmond, 'what's the difference between a fly and a bird?' He clenched his teeth again and pressed on Desmond's neck. Desmond opened his beak.

'I don't know,' Ajay made Desmond say, 'what is the difference between a fly and a bird?'

'A bird can fly, but a fly can't bird!' said Ajay. Desmond flapped his wings and squawked.

The crowd went wild with laughter. A few people clapped in enjoyment. 'That puppet is amazing!' cried one little girl in the front row.

Ajay smiled and looked down at Desmond. This was actually working! 'I say, I say, I say,' he went on, 'what does a vet give to a sick bird?' He pressed again on Desmond's neck and the dodo opened his beak.

'I know this one,' Ajay made the huge dodo say, 'he gives a sick bird ... tweetment!'

The audience laughed heartily yet again. They were enjoying the sight of the blue and yellow feathered 'puppet' so much they didn't even notice that Ajay was moving his lips the whole way through. Ajay told as many bird jokes as he could remember, including a few truly awful ones he had read on the little slips of paper that fall out of Christmas crackers. Each time Desmond played his part perfectly, opening up his beak as Ajay made him talk, waving his wings and wagging his small dodo tail vigorously to make the audience laugh even harder.

Ajay wracked his brains for a bird joke funny enough to give his act the big ending it deserved. 'I have one last joke for you, Desmond,' he said to the bird sitting on his knee, 'and then we'll let the lovely audience recover and catch their breath before the next act.' He thought furiously, what was the best bird joke he ever heard? Whatever it was, he couldn't remember it, so he said, 'I say, I say, I say, Desmond, what did one egg say to the other egg?'

'I don't know,' he made Desmond say, 'what *did* one egg say to the other egg?'

Ajay stood up, holding on to Desmond tightly. 'Let's get cracking!' he shouted. 'Thank you very much, you've been a wonderful audience!'

As the laughing crowd rose to their feet with tears rolling down their cheeks to give him a standing ovation, Ajay grabbed the empty suitcase and darted off the stage, dragging Desmond behind him.

'You were brilliant!' shouted Sam, but Ajay couldn't hear her over the noise of the crowd who were stamping their feet in unison and shouting for more. Desmond looked very proud as Sam petted his head. 'You were brilliant too, Desmond!'

'Well, guys and gals,' said Pat Mustard, 'judging by the audience reaction there can only be one winner tonight. Or do I mean two winners? Laddies and germs, the top prize goes to … Ajay and Desmond the Duck!'

The audience went crazy again, clapping and shouting for Ajay and Desmond. A chant started on one side of the hall of 'Ajay! Ajay! Ajay!' only to be answered by a chant from the other side that went 'Desmond! Desmond! Desmond!'

Sam laughed and chanted along with the 'Ajay!' side as a smiling Ajay gathered the heavy dodo up into his arms again and walked onstage to take a bow and receive the cash prize. Nanny Gigg had pushed her way up to the front of the audience and stood with her fingers in her mouth, whistling loudly. Desmond, in Ajay's arms, fluffed up his blue and yellow feathers and, to roars of approving laughter from the audience, SQUAAAAAAWWWWKKed loudly.

A POSTCARD FROM BRUNO

Hello Nanny and Stink-bag Sam,
I'm enjoying college but there's a really mean girl here who keeps pranking me. Yesterday she filled up an empty crisp bag with thin slices of apple (and you know I hate apples), sealed it up again and left it on my bed. I'd eaten four slices before I realised it wasn't cheese & onion crisps after all. So mean. No news on the monkey egg, I'm bringing it to bed every night and keeping it warm, but no sign of any monkeys yet. Bruno.

CHAPTER EIGHT
A MESSAGE FROM MARJORIE

KNICKERS! KNICKERS!

Beep beep beeep.

KNICKERS! KNICKERS!

Beep beep beeep.

Nanny Gigg turned over in bed and opened her eyes. She reached to her bedside table for her glasses and false teeth but being still half asleep she put the glasses in her mouth and poked the false teeth into her eye. Sitting up and, with the dentures and spectacles on in their proper places, she gave Sindy the budgie a hard stare. Sindy immediately stopped flying in circles around the room and shouting 'KNICKERS' (a particularly unpleasant party piece Bruno had taught her) and fluttered down to perch on top of Nanny Gigg's bedside lamp.

Beep beep beeep.

The beeping noise was still beeping. Nanny Gigg looked around the room for the source of the annoying sound. Her collection of hats and the posters of her favourite rock band, the Roaming Scones, looked back down at her, but none of them were particularly known for their beeping. But still it continued. Beep beep beep.

If Nanny Gigg wasn't mistaken (and, in fairness, she usually was) the noise seemed to be coming from the floor. She spun around in bed like a geriatric gymnast and, hanging over the side, peeped under. Behind the moth-eaten furry slippers and the dust bunnies, up against the back wall, she could see a small red flashing light. Nanny Gigg swiveled around and hopped out of bed. She lay on the floor and reached under the bed, disturbing the dust which tickled her nose and made her want to sneeze. Eventually, after much groping around, her hand landed on a cold metal surface. It felt like it was covered in buttons and switches. The beeping noise became stronger as she pulled it out.

The object was a sandy coloured metal square, around five centimetres thick with two glass screens, one large and one tiny, and rows of knobs at the top and bottom. The bigger screen was lit up and had strange static lines moving down it. Nanny Gigg turned it over in her hands. She had a vague memory of her husband, Daddy Mike, inventing this years ago. Was it called a Talk-Bot 200? 250? Something like that – Nanny Gigg couldn't remember. Daddy Mike was always inventing weird and wonderful things. This one looked very wonderful but also a bit weird, kind of like a smart phone from the years before phones were smart. The object was still making the beeping noise and a red button lit up with every beep. Nanny Gigg pressed the button.

The large screen crackled and lit up fully, as did the smaller screen. In the smaller screen Nanny Gigg could see a flickering image of her own face, and in the larger screen a faded flickering image of ...

'Marjorie Crowe!' exclaimed Nanny Gigg. She sprung to her feet and sat on the side of the bed, clutching the square screen in her hands and looking from the small image of her own smiling face to the smiling face of her old friend on the big screen. This Talk-Bot 200 must have been the 'old-fashioned way' of communication that Marjorie had mentioned in her note!

'Gigg!' said Doctor Marjorie Crowe. 'It's *sooooo* absolutely F.A.B. to see you, darling! You look positively gorgeous. G.O.R-geous!'

Nanny Gigg thought that Marjorie Crowe didn't look too bad herself – she was wearing a big explorer's pith helmet and what looked like a safari shirt with huge, stuffed pockets at the front. Her hair was still jet black and mad curly, just like it had been when they were at school together all those years ago. She was the same age as Nanny Gigg, but her clothes, her bushy hair and her round, smiling face made her look at least ten years younger.

'Did you get my special package?' asked Marjorie. 'I'm so sorry to foist Desmond upon you like that, but my submarine had broken down and I couldn't think of a safer place to send him, especially with your granddaughter being so good with animals. Oh, I *do* hope Desmond hasn't been much trouble?'

'No trouble at all,' lied Nanny Gigg. 'He's been a little feathery angel.' Even Sindy the budgie, now perched on Nanny Gigg's shoulder, squawked scornfully at that fib.

'Oh, goooooood, I'm sooooo happy to hear that. Desmond can be a bit of a handful, the little darling, but I'm soooo glad he's behaving for you.' Marjorie Crowe leaned in towards the camera and her face became bigger in Nanny Gigg's screen. 'Gigg,' she said, her tone more urgent now, 'I've heard rumours that some rather nasty people may be in Dublin at the moment. They go by the name of the Greedy Gourmands. They pretend to be chefs but they are really just animal poachers. And that's a good description for them, because when they catch the animals they tend to cook them and eat them – fried, boiled, roasted or poached! The more exotic the better, and you can't get more exotic than poor old Desmond the dodo. I found him floating on a piece of driftwood in the middle of the Indian Ocean, far away from dry land. I've no idea how he got there or where he came from. All I know is he's a dodo, maybe the last dodo in existence, and it's our job to keep him away from these Greedy Gourmands or whomever else might harm him.'

Sam, woken by the sound of conversation from the next room, knocked on Nanny Gigg's door and walked in rubbing her eyes. Marjorie Crowe spotted her and said, 'Oh Gigg, is that Sam Hannigan? She was only a wee nipper when I saw her last! She's gotten so big!'

Marjorie moved close to the camera again. 'Gigg and Sam, you've got to keep Desmond safely hidden until tomorrow morning. I'll meet you both at Bullock Harbour. You know the little dock near Dalkey? A lovely spot. I'll be there with the *Sea Turtle*. Can you do this for me?'

Sam, now fully awake, answered for them both. 'Keep him safe for one more day? Of course we can do it!'

Marjorie smiled, 'Good girl! I trust you, Sa–' Then the image on the screen of the Talk-Bot 200 flickered, fizzled out and was gone.

It's only another twenty-four hours, thought Sam, *what could possibly go wrong?*

CHAPTER NINE
ARRGH! IT'S A MUMMY!!

In Hannigan's Haven, Sam, Ajay and Nanny Gigg sat at the kitchen table while Desmond the dodo skittered around the kitchen floor on his yellow scaly legs, bouncing from one press door to another. All the other animals in the sanctuary were hiding in their coops, kennels and cages, keeping out of Desmond's way. Even Sindy the budgie had left her usual perch of Nanny Gigg's shoulder and flown to the top of one of the kitchen presses, far out of the reach of the difficult dodo. 'We'll have to take him out somewhere, Nanny,' said Sam, 'he's going crazy again.'

Nanny Gigg took her fingers out of her ears. 'What's that you said, chicken? I couldn't hear you, the dodo is going crazy again. Maybe we'd better take him out somewhere.'

'Good idea,' said Ajay, 'but didn't you say that animal poachers were after Desmond? Where will we go where we can keep him safe?'

'Somewhere indoors maybe, where prying eyes won't see him?' said Sam. 'I've got it! Crazy golf!' She grabbed a copy of the local newspaper, *The Clobberstown Bugle*, off the countertop and flicked through the pages. 'Here it is,' she said, holding up the paper to show them a colourful full-page advert for King Putt's Indoor Krazy Golf. It's just opened up beside the shopping centre at the other side of Clobberstown. It's Egyptian-themed – you know, pyramids and camels and pharaohs and mummies and stuff like that. It's perfect; we can play golf, and Desmond can play around the pyramids!'

The decision was made, and while Nanny Gigg made a pile of cheese sandwiches and a flask of tea and put them into a wicker picnic basket, Sam and Ajay got Desmond dressed up for the outing. Desmond had torn the dinosaur costume to shreds with his beak when they were undressing him after the last trip, so they put Ajay's long blue duffle coat on the dodo, along with Sam's pink wellies. They covered Desmond's head with the wide-brimmed hat that Ajay had worn at the talent show – the brim was so wide that, as long as he kept his feathery head down, you could barely see his long beak beneath it.

To finish off the look, they attached a yellow rubber glove to each of the hanging sleeves of the duffle coat with safety pins. If you looked at Desmond sideways, you'd think he was just a small boy. Dressed as a gangster. Sam hoped that whoever might look at Desmond would look at him sideways.

They piled into Big Bertha, Ajay packing the picnic basket and a plastic sandwich box of his own into the back. Nanny Gigg, wearing her leather pilot's hat again, revved up the engines and drove out of the driveway. As they came through the gates Big Bertha narrowly missed a big cream and red coloured van that was idling outside on Clobberstown Avenue. Ajay thought there was something familiar about the big satellite dish on the van's roof and the black chimneys that came out of its rear end, but he couldn't quite place where he had seen it before ...

CHEESE & CRACKERS, IT'S ...
CAPTAIN STINKY & CHUM

98

As Nanny Gigg drove the short distance to King Putt's, Desmond the dodo leant his head out of the side of the van, much like a dog, and let the wind blow through his feathers.

They pulled up outside the crazy golf building and jumped out of the massive boat-truck. Over the doors of King Putt's there was a picture of a cartoon camel holding a golf club and standing in front of some pyramids. Sam had a quick look up and down the road as Nanny Gigg and Ajay lowered Desmond, in his blue duffle coat and brown hat, out of the big yellow vehicle and, grabbing the picnic basket and Ajay's lunchbox as they went, they hustled the dodo through the doors and into the building.

Sam followed them in, and although she caught an unexpected whiff of fried food on the breeze, she didn't notice the vast cream and red van that came around the corner and parked itself across the road from King Putt's. Even if she did notice it, she wouldn't have thought much of it – apart from the colossal dish and chimneys on the roof, it looked just like an enormous, over-long camper van that a large family might go for their holidays in.

Captain Stinky Derrière sat on the booster seat on the passenger side of the van, holding binoculars up to his eyes as he watched Sam go into King Putt's. 'Monsieur Chum,' he said, turning to his large henchman in the driver's seat, 'ze imbecilic family who 'ave zat tasty-looking dodo 'ave gone into zis King Putt's Krazy Golf. It seems zat we may be shortly playing ze game of golf also. Ze question is, shall we be getting ze 'ole in one, or shall we be scoring a birdie?'

Inside King Putt's, it was so warm that Sam had to take off her jumper as soon as she came in. The blue-haired lady at the desk apologised to Nanny Gigg as she handed over the golf balls and the shortened golf clubs. 'So sorry about the heat. The air conditioning is on the blink, I'm afraid. You can hang your jackets up here on the hooks behind the desk, if you like?' She glanced at Desmond. 'Maybe your little boy would like to take off that big blue duffle coat and that hat? He'll swelter on the course.' Desmond squawked.

'No, thank you,' said Nanny Gigg quickly. 'Little Desmond wants to keep on his coat.' She leaned in and whispered to the blue-haired lady, 'He's going to a surprise fancy dress party this afternoon, and he's dressed up as Paddington Bear.'

Desmond squawked again, even louder this time. The blue-haired lady's eyebrows went up in surprise. 'And don't mind that noise he's making,' said Nanny Gigg. 'It's Peruvian for *Where's my marmalade sandwich?*'

They were relieved to find, when they walked through the pyramid-shaped doors into the miniature golf course, that they were the only customers there that day. The course certainly was Egyptian-themed – every hole had either a pyramid, camels at an oasis, or a creepy mummy's sarcophagus.

Ajay started off at the first hole, a Bedouin tent sitting on a pile of fake sand with a small palm tree beside it. The idea was to get your golf ball to go through the front flap of the tent and out the flaps at the other side and into the hole behind, and Ajay managed to do this on his first stroke. As the ball plopped into the hole, a small magic carpet with a little Aladdin figure rose up over the palm tree on a wire, did a loop-the-loop and landed back down again on the fake sand. Nanny Gigg clapped her hands.

'You're a natural!' said Sam.

'Beginner's luck, I think!' said a very surprised Ajay, who had never even picked up a golf club before. Nanny Gigg and Sam had a go at getting their golf balls through the tent, but neither were as lucky as Ajay, Nanny Gigg making it after four attempts and Sam hitting the ball seven times before it got into the hole.

The next hole was a bit easier – all they had to do was hit the ball up the angled side of a pyramid and into a large opening at the top. The ball then rolled through a tunnel that led out of the other side of the pyramid, where it dropped into a little boat. The boat floated down a small stream of real running water and over a waterfall, where it deposited the ball straight into the second hole. Both Sam and Nanny Gigg managed to do this first time, but poor Ajay had a lot of trouble and ended up wasting twelve strokes. 'I spoke too soon about that beginner's luck,' he said, laughing. 'I'm really falling behind in the scores here!'

'Speaking about falling behind,' said Sam, 'where's Desmond gotten to?' The dodo had wandered off while they were all playing the first hole, sniffing around the miniature pyramids and pecking happily at the plastic camels with his yellow and red beak.

'Ah, I'm sure he's fine,' said Nanny Gigg. 'I can't hear him squawking and I can't hear anything smashing, so he mustn't be up to any of his usual mischief.'

They started on the third hole, a scary-looking stone Egyptian pharaoh's coffin, covered in hieroglyph writing with a mummy's bandaged hand emerging from it. They each placed their golf ball on the starting spot and Ajay raised his golf club to take his first stroke. 'Hold on a minute,' he said, 'if there are only three of us playing, how come I have four golf balls here?'

They looked down at Ajay's feet and, sure enough, there were four golf balls there: Nanny Gigg's orange one, Sam's green one, Ajay's yellow one, and a larger, oddly shaped white one. Sam got down on her knees to have a closer look. It was much bigger than the others, almost three times the size, and it wasn't just pure white – it was covered in small, blue freckly speckles. She prodded it with her finger and the misshapen ball wobbled around crazily in circles. 'This is no golf ball,' said Sam, her ginger eyebrows scrunched up in puzzlement, 'this is an egg!'

'An egg?' said Ajay. 'But we're playing crazy golf in an Egypt-themed indoor miniature golf course – where on Earth would an egg come from?'

There was a quiet squawk from behind them and Desmond the dodo waddled sheepishly from behind a plastic pyramid.

He had shaken off his coat but still wore the big, brown, wide-brimmed hat. He also was wearing what looked like a smirk across his beaky face.

'Kids,' said Nanny Gigg, 'I think that egg … came from that dodo.'
She gulped. 'I think Desmond may actually be a Desdemona!'

'Oh. My. Dog!' said Sam, looking from the big blue-speckled egg to
the large blue-feathered dodo. 'You know what this means? This means
that Desmond the dodo – sorry, Desdemona the dodo – is NOT the last
dodo in the world! This egg isn't just any ordinary egg – it's a BABY
DODO!! This is AMAZING!! This is the most WONDERFUL
thing EVER!!!'

Suddenly there was a rustle and a crash as several plastic palm trees
were knocked over behind them. Sam, Ajay and Nanny Gigg whirled
around to find two men staring at them. One was exceeding tall, with
huge muscled arms and a hairy chest showing through his string vest.
The other was exceedingly short, wearing a grimy chef's hat and a long,
twirly moustache. The small man was holding a crazy golf club which,
though shorter than a normal golf club, was much bigger than him.
The other huge man was holding the smallest dog that Sam had ever
seen – to Sam it looked like a cross between a poodle and a chihuahua.
The tiny dog whimpered as the cross little man began to stamp his
teeny-weeny feet.

'So! It IS a dodo bird!' squeaked the small chef. 'My stupendous
sense of smell never lets me down!' He stared hard at the blue and yellow
dodo and then his gaze fell to the egg at Desdemona's scaly yellow feet.
'Et sacrebleu! What is zis?! An egg? A DODO egg??!' His eyes widened
as his small mouth began to water uncontrollably. 'I 'ave eaten everything

under the sun. I 'ave eaten antelope in Africa, quail in Quebec – I 'ave eaten aardvark in Australia.'

'You have even eaten dinosaur in Dublin, Captain Stinky,' said Chum, 'in the Natural History Museum. Don't you remember? You broke your front tooth on it because it was a stone fossil.' Chum smirked at the thought of it.

'Shut up, Monsieur Chum!' squealed Stinky, stamping his foot again, 'or I will eat your little mutt of a tiny dog too – Foo-Foo will become Food-Food!'

'But first,' he continued, 'I will eat for my dinner zis delectable, delicious, oh-so-rare roast dodo.' He licked his lips. 'And zen for my breakfast I will dine on scrambled dodo egg! For I am Captain Ston-KAY Derrière, ze Greedy Gourmand, and I wish to eat every animal in ze world, alive, dead ... or supposedly extinct! I prefer my meat to be RARE!'

Nanny Gigg and Sam stood in front of Desdemona, their arms stretched out wide to protect her and the dodo egg. Ajay bent down and picked up the lunchbox he was carrying with him. 'The only thing you will be eating,' he said to Stinky, 'is what I have here in my lunchbox.'

'Cheese sandwiches?' smirked the small chef, his moustache curling up in a derisive smile.

'No,' said Ajay, 'live scorpions!'

He opened the lid of the box and flung the two red and black scorpions at Stinky and Chum. Stinky squealed as the first scorpion landed directly on his upturned nose. The other one landed on Chum's chest and immediately crawled through the large holes in his filthy string vest. Chum dropped poor Foo-Foo to the floor and started beating at his vest with his large hairy hands, shrieking loudly.

'Come on,' said Sam, 'let's leg it!'

While Stinky and Chum rolled around on the green carpeted floor, trying to bat the scorpions off, Ajay swooshed Desdemona away and Nanny Gigg carefully put the dodo egg into her wicker picnic basket.

With Sam leading the way, they ran to the emergency exit and pushed it open, emerging from the heat into the cool afternoon air. Within moments they were all safely strapped in to Big Bertha and motoring down the street, back towards Hannigan's Haven, leaving a large cloud of dust behind them.

Stinky and Chum emerged from King Putt's and raced to their van, Foo-Foo following in their wake. 'After zem!' shouted Stinky, and Chum, in the driver's seat, revved the engine and roared down the road in pursuit of Big Bertha.

HOLY MOLEY, IT'S ...
CAPTAIN STINKY & CHUM

ZUT ALORS! THERE IS NO WAY INTO ZIS 'ANNIGAN'S 'AVEN EXCEPT FOR THE FRONT DOOR.

DON'T WORRY, CAPTAIN STINKY, I'M SURE YOU'LL COOK UP A PLAN!

'OW MANY TIMES?! IT IS PRONOUNCED STON-KAY!

HOLD ON, WHAT DID YOU SAY? COOK UP A PLAN?

MONSIEUR CHUM, YOU ARE A GENIUS. PERHAPS I WILL NOT EAT YOUR TINY DOG TODAY.

GRUFF?

IF ZE FRONT DOOR IS ZE ONLY WAY IN, THEN ZIS JUST MIGHT BE ZE KEY. LET US GET COOKING!

109

CHAPTER TEN
TROJAN PIE

Inside Hannigan's Haven, Ajay slowly lowered his binoculars and turned from the window to face Sam and Nanny Gigg. 'You were right, Sam,' he said. 'They *did* follow us.'

'That evil chef with the moustache said he wanted to eat poor old Desdemona,' said Nanny Gigg, 'and the dodo egg. He said he's eaten an aardvark. Who would eat an aardvark, for dog's sake?'

'The weirdest thing I ever ate was a snail,' said Ajay. 'I didn't mean to – I was playing football and I was in goal and it was raining and when the ball was coming towards me I dived for it and I missed and I went face first into a mucky puddle and when I came out of the puddle I was all wet and mucky and I had something crunchy in my mouth and I spat it out and when I looked it was a crushed-up snail shell lying in the grass and under the snail shell was a mushed-up snail and green snail juice was

coming out of it.' He paused, catching his breath. 'Ew,' he said, curling up his face, 'I think I got a bit sick in my mouth a little bit just telling you that.'

'Ajay,' said Sam, 'you're babbling.'

'Yes, Sam,' said Ajay. 'Sorry, Sam.'

'Okay,' said Sam. 'These Greedy Gourmand guys want Desdemona and the egg. We aren't going to give them either.' She lowered her ginger eyebrows and stared hard at Ajay and Nanny Gigg. 'They are going to try to get into the house,' she said, and a smile started to grow on her freckly face. 'I say we let them in – but we will be ready for them.' She banged her fist on the little table beside the sofa. The fishbowl jumped into the air a couple of centimetres and Rover the goldfish popped his head out of the water in surprise.

'It's a pity that Ogg is away today in Wicklow with the Clobberstown scout troop – he would have been more than big enough to take on that Chum character. But we will just have to do it by ourselves,' said Sam. 'Nanny Gigg, gather together as many broomsticks, brush handles, tennis racquets, hockey sticks and hurleys as you can – we've got to block every door.'

Nanny Gigg looked puzzled. 'I thought you said you wanted to let them get in?' she asked.

'Yes,' said Sam, 'but we have to block the doors so they don't get out again! Ajay, I need you to go out to Daddy Mike's shed and see if there are any inventions that might be useful for dealing with small, hungry pests. Make sure all the animals are safely shut in and all happy while you're at it!'

'Gotcha!' said Ajay. He opened the back door and trotted down to the inventing shed. The animals cawed, whinnied and bleated in cheery greeting as he went past. He loved the inventing shed – it was jam-packed with Daddy Mike's amazing gadgets, thingy-ma-jigs and doo-dads from floor to ceiling. No matter how many times he and Sam poked around in there, they always came across some new ingenious invention that they hadn't noticed before.

Sam got a hammer and some nails from under the stairs and helped Nanny Gigg to block off the windows, upstairs and downstairs, with the hockey stocks and broom handles. Then they found the keys for all the

inner doors and locked them, leaving only the door to Nanny Gigg's bedroom unlocked. If the Greedy Gourmand dastardly duo got in, the only way they could go is up the stairs, and the only room they could enter was Nanny Gigg's – they could trap them in there!

They put Desdemona under the stairs, making a nest for her egg out of a laundry hamper filled with Nanny Gigg's most comfortable cardigans. Desdemona was much better behaved now she had the egg to look after, and she sat happily on the pile of pink and green cardigans with the big blue-speckled egg safely tucked underneath her. Sam switched on the little under-stairs light and softly shut the door, bolted it from the outside and pushed an armchair in front of it. With any luck, Stinky and Chum would walk right by the chair without seeing the door and go up the stairs.

Ajay came back in from the inventing shed sneezing, carrying a large cardboard box and pulling a green wheelie bin behind him. 'Holy moley,' he said, 'it's dusty out there.'

'Well,' said Nanny Gigg, 'that shed's been locked up ever since Daddy Mike disappeared all those years ago – the only people who ever go into it are you kids. And Bruno, of course.' She rushed to block up the back door with the last hurley while Ajay opened the box and laid out the contents on the carpet.

'Okay,' he said, 'I took everything that looked like it might be useful. I'm not sure what most of this stuff even does. We've got this Matter Transfer 2000 gadget.' He pointed at a small blue device that looked like a remote control for a toy car with a rubber tube and a funnel attached. 'We have the Freez-Ray 1000' – Ajay held up an object that looked like it was made out of an egg whisk attached to a metal vacuum flask – 'a small bottle of Enorma-Gro 3000 liquid.' Sam winced. She had seen that Enorma-Gro stuff in action before and knew what that little bottle of green liquid was capable of.

'And lastly, but not leastly,' continued Ajay, 'we have this spectacles case thingy which has Mini-Clone 5000 written on the label.'

'What about that wheelie bin?' asked Nanny Gigg. 'Why did you bring that dirty great thing into the house?'

Sindy the budgie, sitting on Nanny Gigg's shoulder, chirped in disapproval at the big plastic bin – even budgies knew that wheelie bins belonged outside, not inside.

Ajay frowned. 'It has a lightning flash on the back and it has a rocket attached to each side. I'm not sure what it does, but it's big enough to fit Desdemona so I thought we could hide her in there if the worst came to the worst.'

'Good thinking, Ajay,' said Sam, 'but leave it down here in the hallway. We'll bring the rest of the stuff upstairs – Nanny Gigg's room will be our base of operations.'

Ajay saluted. 'Sir, yes, sir!' he said, a big smile on his face. Although Ajay was a little scared for the dodo, he was pretty confident that, with the help of Daddy Mike's marvellous inventions, they could repel any intruder. *That is,* he thought, looking at the small pile of dust- and cobweb-covered items on the floor, *if they still work after all these years ...*

Shortly after darkness fell there was a soft knock on the front door. 'The game's afoot,' said Sam quietly. Ajay, Nanny Gigg and Sam had been sitting on the bed in Nanny Gigg's room with only the bedside lamp on, trying to figure out what each of the crackpot inventions Ajay had brought in actually did.

Sam got up and peered out the bedroom window. The cream and red van was still sitting across from the house at the other side of the avenue, lit by the yellow glow of a streetlight. Although the satellite dish on its roof was not moving, the chimneys at the far end were sending out light puffs of white smoke. Sam stood on her tip-toes and stretched her neck to see if she could spot who had knocked on the front door.

'Who is it?' whispered Ajay.

'It's not a *who*, it's a *what*,' replied Sam. 'It's hard to see properly in the darkness, but looks like it might be a great big pie!'

'A big PIE?' said Nanny Gigg. 'What flavour is it?'

'It's a trap!' said Ajay quickly. 'I bet those two exotic animal gobblers are hiding inside!'

Sam turned from the window. 'Of *course* they are,' she said, 'and no matter what flavour that pie is meant to be, we are going to make sure that Captain Stinky Derrière's goose is cooked!'

Sam led Ajay and Nanny Gigg down the stairs and slowly opened the front door. An enormous pie sat on the doorstep. It was circular, two metres wide and at least two metres tall, and seemed to be made of shortcrust pastry. The sides were slightly angled and ribbons of steam rose slowly from the thick crust at the top.

'Oh,' said Sam, as convincingly as she could, 'those two chefs seem to have made us a lovely big pie, how nice of them.' She plucked a handwritten note from where it was taped to the side of the massive pie. 'Listen to this, Nanny Gigg and Ajay,' she said. '*Mes amis, Please accept this humble pie that I and my sous-chef, Monsieur Chum, have baked as an apology for the fright we gave you at the teeny-tiny golf course.*

We are so sorry. We hope you enjoy our pie, we think you will find that it has a verrrrry delicious filling. Bon appétit!'

At that moment there was a cracking-crunching sound as the top of the pie tore off and fell backwards into the garden. A pair of small hands then appeared, digging through the pastry in the side wall of the pie. The hands were followed by the rest of a tiny, crumb-covered man wearing a chef's hat. 'Aha!' cried the small man. 'It is I, Captain Ston-KAY Derrière!' He stepped out of the broken pie crust and into the hallway of Hannigan's Haven, followed closely behind by a huge, hulking, slightly embarrassed-looking man wearing a red bandana and a dirty string vest covered in pie particles.

'Where is your dodo bird and your delicious dodo bird egg?' cried Stinky. 'You will give zem to us now! Tac tac tac!'

'Oh, we'll give it to you all right,' said Sam, ducking down. 'Ajay!' she shouted. 'Let them have it!'

Ajay pointed the Freez-Ray 1000 at Chum and pressed the button on the side. A blue bolt of cold, crackling energy shot off the metal egg whisks and hit Chum straight in the chest. Chum immediately froze and, TIMMMBBBEEERRRRRRRRRR! fell, as stiff as a tree trunk, straight down onto the floor of the hallway. As he fell he knocked into the armchair that Sam had put in front of the door under the stairs, sending it sliding down the hall, and his string vest caught on the doorknob. Chum's weight pulled the door completely out of its frame, revealing a squawking, panicked-looking Desdemona.

'Ze dodo!' squealed Stinky in delight, and, trotting over Chum's dazed and frozen body, made for the space under the stairs.

'Not so fast!' shouted Sam, raising the funnel on the Matter Transfer 2000 and flicking the lever from THERE to HERE. Stinky squealed again as his body seemed to become even smaller and, with a SCHLOOORRRPPPPing noise and a small POPP! he disappeared. Sam pointed the funnel at the front door and flicked the lever from HERE to THERE and Stinky POPPED back into existence, standing beside the door. He looked around in puzzlement and scratched his chef's hat, wondering how he got to the other end of the hall from where the dodo was.

With Stinky safely out of the way, Nanny Gigg reached in under the stairs with both of her bony arms. Gritting her false teeth with effort, she hoisted out Desdemona – laundry hamper, egg and all – and put them in the green wheelie bin. She threw her skinny leg over the side of the bin and climbed in herself, pulling down the green plastic lid. As soon as she did, two big rockets attached to the side of the bin fizzed into life, and the turbo-powered trash can started whizzing down the hallway, directly at Stinky, who flung himself out of the way.

'WHHEEEEEEEE!' cried Nanny Gigg from inside the speeding bin. 'This is *wheelie* fast!'

Stinky jumped to his tiny feet and began to run after the bin, which at this stage had flown over the doorstep and was almost at the garden gate.

'Stinky's flying after the bin!' shouted Sam. 'He's nearly got it!'

Ajay, who had been hunched over another invention, stood up. 'Time that we taught Stinky how to fly for real.' He stepped aside and held his hands over his eyes as forty blue budgies took to the air. They flew down the hallway, out the front door and down the garden, landing in unison on the back of Stinky's white jacket. Bustling each other for space, the forty small budgies dug their claws into the fabric of the chef's coat and flapped their wings as one.

With a whelp of fear Stinky found himself rising up, the air around him vibrating with the rapid motion of forty pairs of beating wings. He squealed as the budgies carried him up over the lampposts and away into the sky, heading towards the Dublin Mountains. As they flew the budgies shouted together, 'Knickers! KNICKERS!!'

'What?' said Sam. 'How??'

Ajay held up a pink case that looked like it should have a pair of Nanny Gigg's spare glasses inside. 'The Mini-Clone 5000,' he said. 'I used it to clone Sindy as many times as I could before it ran out of charge, while you were distracting Stinky and Chum. It's actually too small to clone anything bigger than a budgie!'

There was a commotion from the hallway behind them as Chum roused himself and, shaking his head groggily, spotted Stinky flying high over the skies of Clobberstown. He jumped to his feet, nearly bowling Sam and Ajay over as he ran by them towards the Greedy Gourmand van. With a squeal of rubber tyres on tarmac, Chum drove after Stinky, sticking his head out the driver's side window to follow his boss's path through the sky.

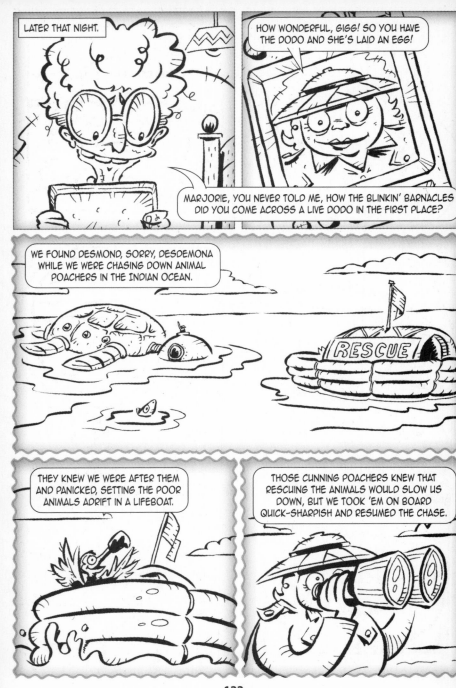

LATER THAT NIGHT.

HOW WONDERFUL, GIGG! SO YOU HAVE THE DODO AND SHE'S LAID AN EGG!

MARJORIE, YOU NEVER TOLD ME, HOW THE BLINKIN' BARNACLES DID YOU COME ACROSS A LIVE DODO IN THE FIRST PLACE?

WE FOUND DESMOND, SORRY, DESDEMONA WHILE WE WERE CHASING DOWN ANIMAL POACHERS IN THE INDIAN OCEAN.

RESCUE

THEY KNEW WE WERE AFTER THEM AND PANICKED, SETTING THE POOR ANIMALS ADRIFT IN A LIFEBOAT.

THOSE CUNNING POACHERS KNEW THAT RESCUING THE ANIMALS WOULD SLOW US DOWN, BUT WE TOOK 'EM ON BOARD QUICK-SHARPISH AND RESUMED THE CHASE.

123

... SO WE BROKE UP THE LIFEBOAT AND PUT A SEA TURTLE LIFEBELT IN WITH THE WRECKAGE, THEN SPREAD AROUND A RUMOUR THAT MY GOOD OLD TRUSTY SUB HAD BEEN SUNK.

SEA TURTLE

WE DON'T KNOW WHERE DESDEMONA CAME FROM, BUT WE'VE NARROWED DOWN OUR SEARCH TO THREE OR FOUR UNCHARTED ISLANDS IN THE INDIAN OCEAN. SO SMALL THEY AREN'T EVEN ON SATELLITE MAPS! SHE MUST BE FROM ONE OF THOSE. WHO KNOWS, THERE MAY BE *ONE OR TWO OTHER DODOS* THERE WAITING FOR HER!

MADAGASCAR

MAURITIUS

REUNION

THAT'S WHY IT'S SO IMPORTANT YOU GET DESDEMONA TO BULLOCK HARBOUR IN THE MORNING, GIGG ...

... WE ARE GOING TO BRING THAT DODO HOME!

124

CHAPTER ELEVEN
THE RETURN OF MR SOFTEE-SUNDAE

As the sun rose over the trees lining Clobberstown Avenue, Sam glanced out the window for the fiftieth time since the skirmish with the Greedy Gourmands the night before. She looked at her watch. 'It's getting late,' she said to Ajay and Nanny Gigg. Both looked bleary-eyed – the three of them had taken turns keeping watch, and none of them had gotten much sleep. 'We better get this dodo to Dalkey.'

'What about that little Stonky fella and his friend, Chump?' said Nanny Gigg, who always got people's names wrong, especially when she didn't like them. 'Won't they be on the lookout for us?'

'I can't see them outside now,' said Sam, 'but Nanny Gigg is right, they will be waiting for us to make a move. We can't take Desdemona to Bullock Harbour in Big Bertha, they would spot us straight away. They might even recognise Ajay's dad's taxi. How are we going to get there?'

Just then there was a knock at the door. Nanny Gigg and Sam froze, staring at each other. Ajay peered out the window and turned back to them looking relieved. 'It's Ogg!'

Sam opened the door and all of them dragged Ogg into the hallway and hugged him. 'Ogg!' cried Nanny Gigg. 'We're so happy to see you, you gorgeous big lug!' Even Sindy, sitting on Nanny Gigg's shoulder, seemed happy to see Ogg and chirruped noisily. 'Shush, Sindy,' whispered Nanny Gigg, and looked up and down the road outside nervously.

They tugged a slightly baffled Ogg into the kitchen and, over three normal-sized mugs of tea and one giant one, told him all about the Greedy Gourmands and their dodo-related transport problems.
Ogg slurped his tea noisily and thought for a couple of seconds.
'Got it!' he said in his deep growly voice. 'Mario Junior Junior!'

'Of course!' said Nanny Gigg. 'Mario Junior Junior could bring us in his Mr Softee-Sundae van – those greedy little gumballs will never notice us!'

Ogg reached into his fur vest and pulled out a mobile phone. He made a quick call, and within a few minutes they heard the unmistakable sound of ice-cream van chimes coming up Clobberstown Avenue. Desdemona was asleep on the laundry hamper with the egg beneath her, so Ogg lifted it out of the front door and down the driveway to the ice-cream van.

Sam, Ajay and Nanny Gigg debated which animal would be the best to bring as a bit of extra muscle, should they run into Stinky and Chum. They decided on Priscilla the python, partly for her strength, length and fierceness, but mostly because she had taken to sleeping in the tall wicker laundry basket from the talent show, so she wouldn't be a problem to transport.

Mario Junior Junior opened the rear door of the Mr Softee-Sundae van so Ogg could bundle Desdemona inside. 'Ciao, pretty lady,' he said to Nanny Gigg as he carefully lifted the hamper, with a sleeping dodo, her precious egg and a bunch of cardigans inside, through the door. 'I hear you wanna go to the seaside?'

Nanny Gigg blushed and adjusted her mop of grey hair and her false teeth. 'That's right, Mario,' she said, as Sam, Ajay and Ogg climbed in after Desdemona. 'Next stop Bullock Harbour!'

But, infuriatingly for Sam and the crew, the next stop for the Mr Softee-Sundae van wasn't Bullock Harbour. Every time they stopped at traffic lights or a yield sign, a small queue of kids lined up at the hatch and Mario Junior Junior hopped out of the driver's seat and started making them ice creams.

All in all it took them an hour and a quarter to make the twenty-minute journey to Dalkey. Sam and the gang were so busy checking their watches during the trip that for a long while they didn't notice a cream and red van with a rotating satellite dish on its roof that was following them at a distance.

As they reached Killiney Hill, Ajay looked out the back window and spotted the Greedy Gourmand van as it rounded a corner behind them. 'We have company!' he shouted.

Mario Junior Junior looked in the rear-view mirror and narrowed his eyes. 'Do not worry, Nanny the Gigg,' he cried. 'I will lose them! Andiamo!'

He put his foot down on the accelerator and the ice-cream van shot off up the hill. Sam, Ajay, Nanny Gigg and Ogg tumbled around in the back, holding on to whatever they could to steady themselves, suddenly very aware that they had no seatbelts. As they rounded a sharp bend,

Ajay grabbed the nearest thing to keep himself from falling – the handle of the whipped ice-cream machine. The delicious goo started to gush out of the machine's spout and squirt all over the floor, making it even harder for the gang to stay upright at all. Desdemona, woken up by the screeching of the van's wheels, hopped out of the hamper and started to eat the dollops of ice cream off the floor and walls with her long beak.

'The egg!' shouted Nanny Gigg and dived for the blue-speckled dodo egg that had fallen from the laundry hamper and was now rolling back and forth across the slippery floor of the ice-cream van. Sam, holding on to a window handle, bent and caught it as it zig-zagged towards her, and cradled it to her chest.

The other van was gaining on them now, and they could see Captain Stinky and Chum in the front seats. Sticking out of Chum's string vest they could just make out the teeny-tiny form of Foo-Foo the poodle-chihuahua. All three of them were covered in the green, red and brown sauces that were splashing crazily around their food van as it chased Mr Softee-Sundae.

Ogg steadied himself and made his way to the whipped ice-cream machine. 'Make cones!' he said to Ajay and Nanny Gigg.

'Make what??' asked Nanny Gigg. 'This is no time for eating ice cream, Ogg!'

'Not eat cone,' said Ogg, pulling the handle and pouring the ice cream onto the wafer to make a perfect ice-cream cone, 'make ice-cream missile!' He took the cone and went to the rear of the ice-cream van. He opened the back window and threw the cone at the Greedy Gourmand van. It splattered on its windscreen and the van swerved from side to side, its window wipers coming on and spreading the cream over the glass.

'More cones!' shouted Ogg, and Nanny Gigg and Ajay made more ice creams, passing them up to Ogg, who chucked them at their pursuers.

Soon the windscreen of the Greedy Gourmand van was completely smeared in a thick layer of ice cream and wafers, and it screeched to a sudden halt at the side of the road. They had lost them! The gang cheered and, turning left at Dalkey village, headed towards Bullock Harbour.

CHAPTER TWELVE
THE BATTLE OF BULLOCK HARBOUR

Bullock Harbour was quiet and peaceful as Mario Junior Junior turned onto Harbour Road and drove down the slope. He parked the ice-cream van at the end of the pier and Sam, Ajay, Nanny Gigg and Ogg looked out the serving hatch at the side. There was no sign of either Doctor Marjorie Crowe or her *Sea Turtle* submarine. A couple of seagulls flapped down near the van and stalked around on the paving stones, eyeing it hungrily, but other than that there was no movement at all on the small pier.

Suddenly there was a screeching sound and the Greedy Gourmand van came around the corner at the top of Harbour Road. It sat there revving its engines for a moment and then started to drive down the hill at a very slow pace. It turned onto the pier and kept going directly towards them, slowly but surely, its engines making a loud noise in the still air.

'Guys,' said Sam, still holding the dodo egg to her chest, 'they aren't stopping.'

She was right – the cream and red van, its windscreen so covered in sticky ice cream that they couldn't see the driver and passenger behind it, moved relentlessly toward them. There was a **KLANG** and a KRUNCH as the front of the Greedy Gourmand van met the side of the Mr Softee-Sundae one and Sam and the gang were jolted around inside. The smaller ice-cream van started to move sideways under the pressure and its tyres squealed as they slid sideways on the pier.

'We're being pushed towards the edge!' shouted Ajay. 'Get out! Get out!'

Sam and Nanny Gigg opened the back door and jumped out, landing on the stone pier. They were followed by Ogg, who carried Desdemona under his huge, hairy arm, and Ajay, who had the laundry basket with Priscilla the python inside.

Mario Junior Junior was the last out, leaping from the driver's door as the ice-cream van, with a squeal of tyres and a smell of burning rubber, toppled over the edge of the pier. 'My lovely van!' he cried, distraught.

With a belch of black smoke from its chimneys, the Greedy Gourmand van finally came to a shuddering halt. The front doors swung open and Captain Stinky Derrière hopped down onto the pier, twiddling his elaborate moustache. He was followed by the lumbering form of Mister Chum, who was holding his tiny dog, Foo-Foo. All three were covered in a variety of sauces and smelled strongly of curry.

'Aha,' said Stinky, wiping something green from his forehead with a little white hanky, 'now I 'ave you!'

He pointed his tiny finger at Sam. 'You, ginger-haired girl, will give me ze dodo egg,' he ordered, then he pointed at Ogg, 'and you, big hairy man-person, will give me zat delicious dodo.'

'No way, no how,' said Sam. 'This dodo is a very precious thing – it's something we thought we had lost forever and it's somehow, by some miracle, been given back to us. We are lucky to have Desdemona and even luckier that she has her egg. It's a second chance for us, don't you see? A second chance for us humans to get it right.'

'Second chance, schmecond schmance,' said Stinky, wrinkling up his moustache. 'Get zem, Chum!'

Chum, looking a little reluctant, made a half-hearted run directly at Ogg, who laid Desdemona and her egg carefully on the ground and casually reached into his furs. He took out four stone axes with wooden handles which he flung, one by one in quick succession, at Chum. With a deafening noise of four metallic KLANGGGS, Chum suddenly and unexpectedly found himself stuck to the side of the Greedy Gourmand van, pinned in place by axes that stuck right through the fabric of his dirty string vest and his filthy chequered chef's trousers.

Foo-Foo, emerging from his vest, bit Mister Chum on the finger and ran towards Ogg, who nimbly picked her up and petted her. She gave a small, happy bark.

Captain Stinky let out a high-pitched roar of rage and, taking a sharp, glittering knife and fork from under his chef's hat, ran directly at Desdemona. Stinky's eyes were crazed and a long dribble of drool hung off his lips as he ran. 'Zat delicious, delectable dodo will be mine!' he screamed as he ran, licking his lips with his tiny tongue.

Quickly, Ajay took the pungi pipe from his jacket pocket and tossed it to Sam. He kicked over the tall laundry basket and shouted, 'Blow, Sam! Give us a charming tune!'

Sam caught the flute deftly with one hand and, cradling the dodo egg in the other, put the mouthpiece of the pungi pipe to her lips and blew. A beautiful, haunting note emerged from the pipe and floated high into the sunny seaside air.

On the ground in front of Stinky, the tall laundry basket jerked slightly to one side and, with a slithering sound, the long body of Priscilla the python emerged, answering the call of the snake-charmer's flute. Stinky tried to stop running but his teeny feet slid on the smooth stones of the pier, propelling him straight into the wide open mouth of the gigantic snake. 'That dodo is mine ...' he began to shout, but his furious, squeaky yell was cut short by a CLOMMPPing noise as Priscilla snapped her gargantuan jaws shut. Now it was the enormous python's turn to lick her lips, turning her head to admire the Stinky-shaped lump in her middle.

Just then there was a mighty WHOOOOOOSSSHHHHHing noise and a massive spray of water. Sam and Ajay turned to see the *Sea Turtle* submarine surfacing at the side of the pier with, to Mario Junior Junior's delight, the Mister Softee-Sundae van safe and unharmed on its deck.

The submarine was a fantastic sight, sea-green in colour with a curved blue hull in the shape of a giant turtle. A hatch opened up at the top and Doctor Marjorie Crowe, wearing a pith helmet and a sand-coloured safari jacket, popped out her head. 'Ahoy there, shipmates! Anyone fancy a trip?'

A POSTCARD FROM SAM

Sandwich Harbour
WALVIS BAY, NAMIBIA

Hi Bruno,
As you can see we decided to take a bit of a holiday while you are at Irish college. We are off to the Indian Ocean in a brillo submarine that belongs to one of Nanny Gigg's friends. We have a delivery to make there, then we'll be back in time to meet you when you get back from college. Hopefully. Wish you were here. (I actually do, it's brilliant!)
Sam. x

CHAPTER THIRTEEN
HOME SWEET HOME?

In the two weeks since they had left Bullock Harbour – after having waited for the Guards to take away a very remorseful Chum and a slimy Stinky, freshly sneezed out of Priscilla's belly, and having waved a thankful goodbye to Ogg and Mario Junior Junior at the quayside – Sam, Ajay and Nanny Gigg had seen many more wonderful sights. From the deck and the viewing windows of Marjorie's magnificent *Sea Turtle* submarine, they had seen pods of cute dolphins, who followed the ship for kilometres, clicking and squeaking. They had seen breathtaking schools of huge blue whales, the largest mammal on Earth, splashing in the water playfully, like gigantic puppies. They had passed through underwater forests of brightly coloured jellyfish, their long tentacles hanging down like rubbery ropes that swished and danced in the wake as the *Sea Turtle* passed by.

Every day since they had rounded the Cape of Good Hope in South Africa and entered the Indian Ocean, Marjorie had been up on deck with her binoculars, searching for uncharted islands. She was also on the lookout for the evil animal poachers. The *Sea Turtle* was speedy enough to outrun any poacher's ship, but even so, Marjorie had insisted that Desdemona stay safely below deck. Besides that, Marjorie reckoned,

Desdemona had something precious to keep safe and warm herself –
her dodo egg.

On the fourteenth day of the voyage, after they had passed the islands
of Madagascar and Mauritius and were way out in open water, Sam, Ajay
and Nanny Gigg were below deck in the *Sea Turtle's* galley, boiling the
kettle for a cup of tea when Marjorie called from above. 'Ahoy! Gigg!
Kids! We may have found something!'

Abandoning their tea and rushing up on deck, they found Marjorie standing with her binoculars clamped to her eyes and a huge, beaming smile on her face. 'There!' she cried, over the sound of the *Sea Turtle's* engines. 'A tiny island! Can you see it?'

They looked in the direction she was pointing, straining their eyes, but couldn't see anything at first. Then, as the *Sea Turtle* followed the course of Marjorie's finger, they gradually made out a small dot on the horizon. A small dot that became a small green lump, surrounded by water. A small green lump that became an island, thick with palm trees, with a foliage-covered mountain and a wide, yellow-sanded beach.

'This island doesn't appear on maps and it's too small to show up on satellite imaging,' said Marjorie as Desdemona waddled across the deck to stand beside her. 'It has no name, Desdemona. Or does it? Is it called … home?'

Desdemona squawked.

They docked the *Sea Turtle* as close as they could to the yellow sandy beach and brought out a small, inflatable dinghy. They got into the dinghy, carefully lowered Desdemona, her laundry hamper nest and the egg into it, and rowed to the shore.

As Sam got out of the dinghy and waded through the gentle surf onto the beach, she was struck by how quiet the island was. There were no human sounds other than their own breathing, no sound of machinery or cars or trucks. And there was certainly no sound of the Greedy Gourmand exotic animal food van. To Sam, it looked like paradise. She breathed the fresh, sweet island air through her freckly nose and deep into her lungs, closing her eyes.

Ajay helped Desdemona out of the dinghy and carried her to the sand, Marjorie and Nanny Gigg following behind carrying the laundry hamper with Nanny Gigg's cardigans and the egg.

Desdemona, her feet on the sand, waddled forward onto the beach and let out a loud SQUAAAWWWKK. She looked expectantly at the green treeline where the island jungle met the beach, her long yellow and red beak turning left and right. There was no answer, only silence. Desdemona the dodo's blue-feathered head sank down low.

Then the silence was broken by a small cracking noise. Desdemona let out another squawk and they turned to see the dodo egg, sitting on top of Nanny Gigg's comfy green and pink cardigans, begin to break open from the inside. Desdemona waddled to the side of the hamper as a tiny beak broke through the side of the blue-speckled eggshell. A tiny

beak that was followed by the tiny body of a baby dodo! It let out a tiny squawk and Desdemona squawked herself, hopping up and down on her yellow scaly feet and flapping her wings for joy.

She's not the only dodo in the world anymore, thought Sam, hugging the big blue and yellow bird as it squawked loudly in glee.

The dodo's happy squawks seemed to echo down the beach, the sound bouncing off the treeline as if answering her. Desdemona froze in her joyful dance, listening with her blue head cocked at an angle. The squawking noise from the treeline kept on going, getting louder and louder. This was no echo!

Suddenly the vegetation at the treeline exploded as dozens and dozens of blue and yellow bodies erupted from the jungle and waddled onto the beach.

'DODOS!!' shouted Sam.

'Aye,' said Marjorie, wiping tears from her eyes, 'there be dodos here!'

Soon they were surrounded by blue and yellow feathery dodos of all shapes and sizes, squawking loudly in greeting, welcoming their friend Desdemona home and celebrating the birth of her baby dodo.

Nanny Gigg and Ajay hugged each other, laughing. Sam hugged Desdemona gently one last time before the big blue bird waddled off to meet her friends.

Sam wiped a tear off her freckly cheek. She knew she could never tell anyone about this wonderful place, but she didn't care – for the sake of the dodos, this was a secret she would never share, and an adventure she would never forget.

'Welcome home, Desdemona,' she said, 'Welcome to Dodo Island.'

A (FINAL) POSTCARD FROM BRUNO

ALSO BY
AUTHOR & ILLUSTRATOR
ALAN NOLAN

The worst U12s hurling team in Ireland want you! Join Fintan, Rusty, Katie and team mascot Ollie the Dog as they recruit new players, learn new skills and try to thwart the efforts of a rival manager to steal the peculiarly precious Lonergan Cup!

www.OBrien.ie

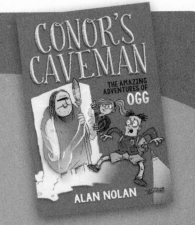

When best pals Conor and Charlie accidentally uncover a prehistoric man frozen in a block of ice, life suddenly gets a bit TOO interesting!

Pre-hysterical fun from Alan Nolan.

www.OBrien.ie

IT'S ALL GOING TO THE DOGS!

Animal lover Sam Hannigan is having a truly woof week.

She and her best friend Ajay were messing around with the Brain Swap 3000 – one of her grandad's crackpot inventions – and now Sam is stuck inside the body of her neighbour's dog!

Barking-crazy adventure from Alan Nolan.

www.OBrien.ie

FOR MORE INFO, VISIT
WWW.OBRIEN.IE

Alan Nolan lives and works in Bray, County Wicklow,
Ireland. He is co-creator (with Ian Whelan) of *Sancho* comic
which was shortlisted for two Eagle awards, and is the
author and illustrator of *The Big Break Detectives Casebook*,
the 'Murder Can Be Fatal' series, *Fintan's Fifteen*, *Conor's Caveman*,
Sam Hannigan's Woof Week and the Irish World Book Day 2019
novel *Sam Hannigan's Rock Star Granny*.

Many thanks to Nathan Browne ('It is pronounced Ston-KAY!') and
to the random little girl in the random library that time who blurted
out the best phrase I had heard in years: 'monkey eggs'.

Special thanks to my fantastic editor Nicola Reddy,
and to Michael O'Brien, Emma Byrne, Ivan O'Brien
and all at The O'Brien Press.

And extra-special thanks, as ever, to my long-suffering family,
Rachel, Adam, Matthew and Sam.

WWW.ALANNOLAN.IE

WWW.OBRIEN.IE

From tots to teens and in between!

Visit **www.obrien.ie** for more brilliant books from
The O'Brien Press

Discover your next adventure today with our wide
range of children's books from great authors.

There's something for readers of all ages – historical fiction,
picture books, sport, graphic novels, young adult fiction
and lots more!

Read a sample chapter from one of our books or watch an
author video – and make sure to keep an eye out for special
offers and competitions.

Just for schools:

We have hundreds of resources for schools, including
teaching guides and activity sheets, all created by teachers for
teachers to make it so easy to bring our novels into your classroom.

All FREE to download today!